RONIN'S RETURN

HEARTS & HEROES SERIES BOOK #3

ELLE JAMES

TWISTED PAGE INC

RONIN'S RETURN

HEARTS & HEROES SERIES BOOK #3

New York Times & USA Today
Bestselling Author

ELLE JAMES

EBOOK ISBN-13: 978-1-62695-089-4

ISBN Print: 978-1-62695-084-9

This book is dedicated to Italy and the wonderful visits I've had in that fabulous country. I love the history, the language, the architecture, the people and the wine. And to Venice, a city of love and intrigue. Thank you for being such a great place to vacation!

AUTHOR'S NOTE

Enjoy other military books by Elle James

Hearts & Heroes Series
Wyatt's War (#1)
Mack's Witness (#2)
Ronin's Return (#3)
Sam's Surrender (#4)
Brotherhood Protector Series
Montana SEAL (#1)
Bride Protector SEAL (#2)
Montana D-Force (#3)
Cowboy D-Force (#4)
Montana Ranger (#5)
Montana Dog Soldier (#6)
Montana SEAL Daddy (#7)
Montana Ranger's Wedding Vow (#8)
Montana Rescue

Visit ellejames.com for more information
For hot cowboys, visit her alter ego Myla Jackson at
mylajackson.com
and join Elle James and Myla Jackson's Newsletter at
http://ellejames.com/ElleContact.htm

CHAPTER 1

WHAT WERE the chances of finding her in such a twisted city, with all its alleyways going nowhere and canals slipping between centuries-old buildings? With Carnival just kicking off, Ronin Magnus couldn't have chosen a worse time to visit Venice.

He didn't know if he'd find Isabella, but he knew he had to try. If for no other reason than to get her out of his mind.

Ronin stepped off the train with hundreds of other tourists eager to experience Venice, some for the first time and all for the annual celebration of Lent. Like them, a current of excitement and anticipation coursed through his veins at seeing the City of Love. But this wasn't his first time in Venice.

Two years ago, during his last real vacation, he'd roamed the streets and canals of Venice and met a woman. Two years had passed since he'd seen her. In those two years, he had neither seen nor heard from her. But she existed in every waking and sleeping dream.

Enough was enough.

Ronin had come to debunk the love part of the Venice equation.

His mission? Find the woman who haunted his dreams and fantasies and prove to himself the haunting attraction was all just a dream he'd blown out of proportion.

Then maybe he could get on with his life, enjoy other women and forget about her.

With purpose in his step, he headed for Piazza San Marco with its little sidewalk café. It was there he'd had his first real date with Isabella and his last. There, they'd kissed and said their goodbyes. So there, he'd begin his search.

He had nothing but her first name to go on. She'd been secretive about where she lived and what her last name was. They'd met at a masquerade ball in a palatial mansion, one of the oldest in the city, owned by a multi-millionaire with worldwide business interests, based out of Italy. Once a year, the tycoon opened his Venetian mansion to the city, inviting any and all who cared to attend during Carnival.

That fateful day two years ago, Ronin had come with one of his SEAL buddies, hoping to meet women. He'd been skeptical about the masquerade part, opting for a simple pirate's costume.

She'd dressed as a female version of a masked high-wayman or bandit, complete with a sword in a scabbard slung at her waist. Her jet-black hair spread out about her shoulders, hanging in waves down her back to her waist. She'd stood at the top of a sweeping staircase, her feet spread apart, hands on her hips, and her chin tilted upward, as if in challenge.

All the lovely ladies wearing colorful ball gowns suitable for the 1800's seemed to fade into the background as Isabella walked down the stairs, every step confident, her swaying movements, catlike in grace, and sexy beyond anything Ronin had ever imagined.

He'd stood transfixed, unable to tear his gaze from her. As if carried in a dream, Ronin moved, intercepting her at the base of the stairs.

She'd paused before reaching the bottom and stared down her nose, speaking in musical, if haughty, Italian.

When he shook his head, she switched to Spanish then French.

Ronin shook his head and watched as her brows above the mask wrinkled. Then she smiled, her blood-red lips curving upward. "English."

"How did you guess?"

Isabella snorted softly. "It was the blank look in your eyes and the moronic expression on your face." Despite her insult, her voice was melodic, husky and sexy as hell.

It tugged Ronin low in the groin, sending heat waves throughout his body. "Nice. Your grasp of English is excellent. I barely hear the Italian accent."

She shrugged. "I had an American tutor. My father insisted I learn American English." She frowned and waved her hand. "Please step aside. If I must be here, the least I can do is dance."

Ronin held out his hand. "Dance with me." The words came out more as a command than as a question.

"And why should I dance with you?" she'd asked.

"Because I asked?"

"No, you did not ask. You demanded."

"Would a pirate ask a damsel to dance?" He fisted his hands on his hips and blocked her path.

She stared hard with eyes such a pale blue they could have been glacial ice. "Would a bandit capitulate without a fight?"

"Perhaps, if she were the least bit attracted to the pirate."

"Rest assured, I'm not the least bit attracted to you or any other pirate in the room."

Ronin winced. "You wound me." He was far too attracted to her, for his own good and her rejection was like a gauntlet thrown in his face. He wasn't giving up yet. "Ah, fair maiden," Ronin lifted a single finger, "you are not attracted because you have yet to dance with a pirate."

"I've danced with enough clowns to be permanently crippled. Why should I dance with you, a complete stranger?"

"Because you crave danger and the thrill of the unknown. And because you think I'm cute." He graced her with a wink and a sexy smile. "So, what do you say? Dance or stand here all night. Either way, I'm getting to know this beautiful bandit."

Her eyes narrowed. "How do you know I am beautiful? A mask can hide a great deal."

"Beauty doesn't have to be physical. Perhaps I find

beauty in your attitude and the way you owned the room when you stood on the landing above. You exude the strength of an Amazon warrior."

Again, she snorted. "Some men find strong women intimidating and unattractive."

"Those men are fools."

She tilted her head. "Again, why should I dance with you?"

"So I won't get a pain in my neck staring up at you on the stairs?" He offered his hand. and lowered his voice. "Go on. Take a chance."

She hesitated for a very long moment. "I could ask one of the guards at the door to escort you out of the ballroom."

"But then you'd never know what you'd missed. I could be the best dancer you've ever had the pleasure of dancing with."

"Or the worst." Her lips pursed and her eyes narrowed.

He nodded. "Or the worst."

With a sigh, she laid her hand in his and descended those last two steps. She wasn't short, but the top of her head only came up to his shoulder.

A perfect fit. He lifted her hand to press a kiss to the back of her knuckles.

"You are a bold man, taking liberties."

"I'll take more than that, if you let me." With her hand in his, he spun her out and back into the crook of one arm, and then dipped her low. "Are you ready for an adventure?"

She stared up at him. "Yes. But don't get carried away. I have a sword, and I'm not afraid to use it."

He laughed out loud and, before he could think better of it, he crushed his lips to hers in a brief, heat-infused kiss. Then he brought her back to her feet and waltzed her around the ballroom until the music changed into a sensuous slow dance.

"What is your name, fair bandit?" he asked, pulling her closer.

She rested her cheek against his chest. "Isabella," she whispered.

He leaned back and stared into her ice-blue eyes. "I would have pegged you for a Dianne or Katherine, not such a sweet name as Isabella."

She shrugged. "I am sorry to disappoint."

"No, you're not a disappointment. An enigma." By that time, they were close to the entrance to the ballroom and the building.

She looked up. "Want to get out of here?" Behind the mask, her eyes danced with mischief and excitement.

"As long as you're coming with me," he'd answered.

"Then on my count, we make a run for the door."

He arched an eyebrow. "Why don't we just walk out?"

"We're fugitives—a pirate and a bandit. The authorities would have us hanging from the yardarm. Are you with me?" She slipped her hand into his.

He chuckled. "On your count."

She glanced left and right. "Three, two, one...go!" Her hand tightened in his, and she ran for the door, slipping behind a large potted plant to avoid detection from the sentry standing guard.

Once outside, she didn't stop running until she'd led him through several narrow alleys to an arched portico, dead-ending onto a canal.

"Are you sure you didn't pick a pocket or steal some rich woman's jewels?" he asked, coming to a stop in time to keep from falling into the murky water.

"I'm sure. What need have I of jewels? The stars in the sky are all the diamonds a woman could ever want."

Ronin had stood at the edge of the canal and pulled her into his arms. "You truly are a mystery. A beautiful woman at a masquerade ball, who doesn't care for fancy dresses or jewelry." He shook his head and pressed a kiss to her forehead. "Where have you been all my life?"

Her burst of laughter echoed off the arched portico. "Is that the best line you could come up with, English?"

"You steal the words from my mind. All I can do is speak from my heart." He bent to nibble the soft skin beneath her earlobe. "Where do we go from here, my sweet bandit?"

She drew in a deep breath and let it out. "I'll show you." Leaning up on her toes, she brushed his lips with hers. Then she stepped away from him and jumped over the ledge.

Ronin's heart leaped into his throat until she popped her head over the ledge.

"Are you coming or not?" She held the line for a black lacquer gondola, the interior lined in deep red paint.

He hesitated. "You really are a thief?"

Her smile spread across her face. "It's not stealing if you bring it back. I'm only borrowing it for a little while." With a furtive glance, she waved him forward. "Come on."

"Geez, how am I going to explain to my commander why I'm in jail in Italy?"

She shook her head. "Don't worry. I'll take all of the blame. Now, are you coming, or am I going on a romantic boat ride alone?" Her raised eyebrows issued the challenge.

His libido accepted. How could a red-blooded military man walk away from a beautiful woman and the promise of romance on the canals of Venice? *Not this Navy SEAL.*

Ronin jumped down to the launch and stepped into the boat. It rocked gently. Familiar with keeping his balance in watercraft, he steadied the rocking before he held out his hand to Isabella.

She tossed in the line and laid her fingers in his. When she stepped into the boat, her foot must have caught on the edge. She pitched forward and crashed into him.

For a moment, he thought they'd both end up in the murky water of the canal, but he leaned to one side, taking her with him and landing on the bottom of the boat.

His body cushioning her fall, she lay sprawled across him.

"I am so sorry." Isabella pushed against his chest, rising to straddle his hips. She yanked the mask from her face and stared down at him, her brow puckered, blue eyes narrowed in concern. "Are you all right?"

Moonlight shone down from above, bathing her face in a soft blue glow.

The fall and subsequent landing had nothing to do with his inability to catch his breath.

Isabella stole his breath away.

"Talk to me, English. Tell me you're okay." She lay back down and pressed her ear to his chest. "Are you breathing?" she asked. "Your heart still beats. Why won't you answer me? What have I done to you?"

"Sweetheart," Ronin started, then cleared his throat and tried again. "You're doing crazy things to me." He cupped her cheeks in his palms and raised her face so he could look into her eyes. "And if you don't get up soon, you'll know exactly what effect you're having on me."

Her eyebrows rose up her forehead, and she swept her tongue across her lips. "Oh." As she shifted, her cheeks flushed darker. "I can't seem to..." Isabella rocked on his hips, struggling to get her feet beneath her.

Her movements exacerbated his desire. His groin tightened, and he hardened beneath her.

Ronin gripped her arms. "Be still, woman," he said through gritted teeth.

"I'm sorry." She continued to shift her bottom against his crotch. "I can't get my feet..."

"And I can't take much more of this." He dragged her down and claimed her mouth in a deep, mind-blowing kiss. With his tongue, he traced the seam of her lips until she parted them, letting him inside.

Their tongues thrust and caressed in a primal dance.

When his lungs were starved, and he had no choice but to come up for air, he lifted her off his body and sat her on the bench. As much as he wanted her, he wouldn't make love to her in the bottom of a boat.

Her eyelids drooped, and she held onto his arms to steady herself. Finally, she let go and touched a hand to her lips. "I am sorry for my clumsiness. I am sure I have not impressed you with my grace."

"I don't think you could be any more perfect." He rose to his feet and looked around. "I don't suppose there are oars?"

Isabella laughed, the sound musical and light. "The boat masters use a pole to maneuver the waterways."

Ronin frowned. "If I'm poling, how romantic will that be? And don't ask me to sing. Whatever might be starting between us will quickly end."

She smiled. "Just pole. I'll let you know where to turn."

"Not the fastest getaway vehicle," he muttered. "We'd better hope we aren't chased by the water police, driving their jet boats." He located the long black pole moored to hooks affixed to the side of the boat, raised the point up in the air and dug the end into the water until the tip touched bottom. The gondola moved forward.

"Slow where the waterways cross," she warned him.

As he familiarized himself with the movements needed to propel the small craft through the canals, Ronin relaxed.

In the distance, perhaps on another watery street,

the deep rich sound of a man singing echoed off the centuries-old buildings.

Soon, Isabella hummed in tune with the song. Then she whispered the words, her Italian soft and achingly beautiful.

Her words and her song flowed like the boat, past docks, doors and alleyways, filling the darkness with a haunting melody. She fit directions in English between the lilting Italian. When the song came to an end, she said, "Stop at the next pier."

So caught up in her melody, Ronin almost missed her instruction. He dug the pole into the silt at the bottom of the canal and brought the little boat to a halt a couple feet past the dock. In seconds, he backed up and brought the gondola alongside the pier. While he once again stowed the pole on the hooks along the side of the boat, Isabella tied the line on the mooring of the pier.

Ronin lifted her out of the boat onto the wooden dock then leaped up beside her and looked at the shadowed building in front of them. "What is this place?"

She shrugged. "I think it's an old apothecary. But this isn't the place I wanted to take you. Let's go before anyone sees us." Slipping her hand into his, she turned toward an alley.

He held her back, digging in his heels. "Who are you afraid will see us?"

She didn't look him straight in the eye. Instead, she stared at the alley, as if willing Ronin to blindly follow, no questions asked. "Why the police, of course. You don't want to get caught with a stolen boat, do you?"

Ronin chuckled. "*Now,* she worries about getting caught with stolen goods." He started toward the alley, his hand curling tightly around hers. "Where are we going?"

"It's a surprise," she called over her shoulder.

"Probably taking me to her pimp to have me stripped of all my money and credit cards," he muttered.

"I heard that. I don't need your money or credit cards. Now, be quiet and hurry."

Soon she stopped in front of an old building with brass handles on dark-stained doors and a third-floor balcony with wrought iron railing, overlooking the street.

"Where are we?" he asked.

She smiled and pushed open the door. "Welcome to Hotel Eden."

Ronin vividly recalled everything from that night. From dancing at the masquerade ball, the gondola and her voice—and making love for the first time in Eden. The following three days passed like a dream. They'd spent the days holed up in Hotel Eden, making love in the sunlight streaming through the window of their room and most of the way through the next night. They didn't leave the tiny hotel, preferring to have a nearby restaurant deliver their food.

By the time his vacation had come to an end, Ronin was head over heels in love with the beautiful Isabella. He'd even considered leaving the Navy to stay in Italy with her. But when he'd broached the matter of the future, she'd changed the subject, kissed him, or took off another item of clothing. His leave came to an end and he was due to fly back to Virginia the fourth afternoon.

They'd had lunch in the Piazza San Marco at the little bistro café. She'd worn a tie-dyed sundress, a broad-brimmed hat and sunglasses she'd picked up from a street vendor on one of their few outings the day before.

He'd asked her to remove the glasses so he could see her beautiful blue eyes.

She'd refused, claiming she didn't want him to see her cry.

Now, two years later, he stood in the crowded Piazza San Marco, desperately searching for that broad-brimmed hat, her coal-black hair or her ice-blue eyes.

The café was still where it had been. The name had changed, but the same tables stood outside the little shop, two years older, but the same.

Tourists wandered around the wide-open square, feeding pigeons and coaxing them to land on their arms and hands in exchange for a treat. A jumbo-tron media screen had been erected on one end of the square for the Carnival festivities as it had been two years ago.

On the surface, nothing had changed.

But Ronin had.

He'd been deployed several times. The buddy he'd come with to Venice had been killed during one of the operations, and time had passed.

He'd come to put the ghost of Isabella and their magical time together to rest, once and for all.

First, he had to find her. As he stared at the bistro tables filled with tourists, he searched for a flash of blue eyes or long black hair, hanging over one shoulder.

The number of tables outside the café had increased to at least double what had been there on his last visit. He took his time, running his gaze over every guest of the café, praying luck would be on his side.

As his gaze slipped over every occupant, hope faded. No one even came close to resembling her. The crowd in the square was too thick to allow him to find anyone. Why he'd thought he could just waltz into Venice during Carnival and find one woman... He shook his head.

He'd just about given up and turned to walk away when a movement in the far corner of his eye caught his attention. The jumbo-tron had been turned on, displaying images of the people milling about the piazza.

Ronin looked up in time to see a woman wearing a pale blue Pashmina scarf around her face.

Though her face was hidden for the most part, there was something about the way she held her head, and the way she kept turning, that caught his attention. Her glances darted, as if she was expecting someone to show up, perhaps someone she didn't want to see.

His pulse pounding, his throat clenching, Ronin glanced at the jumbo-tron and the buildings displayed in the background. Could it be her? Could she really be in the square full of people? The chances were one in a million, but he had to know.

Keeping an eye on the huge display screen, he

worked his way through the crowd. There was the jester on stilts and the woman in the flamboyant purple dress. But where was the woman with the pale blue scarf?

A tall man, Ronin could see over most people, most of the time, but this was Carnival. The costumes were outlandish and bigger than life. Hats blocked his view. If not for the large screen with its view from above the crowd, he'd be searching for a needle in a brightly colored haystack.

Finally, he found a woman in a light-colored scarf and pushed his way through the crowd to get to her. Out of breath from excitement more than exertion, he touched her shoulder. "Isabella?"

The woman turned, her face coming into focus.

Ronin's heart plummeted to his knees.

"*Scusami?*" The woman had white hair, tucked beneath the blue scarf. Wrinkles lined her face, and her eyes were brown, not blue.

"Excuse me." He cleared his throat. "My mistake."

She smiled and waved her hand, encompassing the crowd. "*Nessun problema. Buona giornata.*"

Ronin stepped back, the excitement of moments before drained from his body and soul. He was crazy to think he'd find her here. With so many people crowding the city, he'd be lucky to find his hotel, much less one woman whose last name he'd never learned. He turned toward one of the piazza's exits, intent on finding his way to his hotel.

"Ronin?" a familiar voice said behind him.

He spun and stared into the face of the woman who'd haunted him ever since the last time they'd met.

CHAPTER 2

Isabella Pisano had spent the past hour, trying to lose her bodyguards. How did she tell her father she knew how to take care of herself, and she didn't need bodyguards to follow her around? What she needed was space away from the oppressiveness of the constant supervision she'd endured since her return to Venice.

Because her father was a very wealthy man, he felt compelled to keep his family safe from kidnappers. Isabella was a prime target for those who would dare to capture and use her in trade for a hefty ransom.

She missed the freedom she'd had over the past year away from Venice, away from her life as a debutante and spoiled little rich girl. Isabella craved the independence and purpose she'd gained in her year away from Venice.

Slipping free of her bodyguards hadn't been too difficult in the crowded streets. With so many visitors in Venice for the annual Carnival celebration, she'd easily switched her bright red scarf for a pale blue one and tucked her hair beneath the folds.

Alone at last, she wandered the streets, remembering another time, two years ago when she'd slipped free of her father's men in order to spend time with a man who had made her blood hum and her heart race. Two years ago, she'd made the mistake of letting a man into her heart and bed, knowing nothing could ever come of it. She had been on the verge of an entirely different path in her life. Having taken a female refugee into the Pisano household, she'd learned of the plight of women and children in Syria, and had vowed to make a difference.

She hadn't had time to follow her lover, nor had he offered to take her with him. Had he offered, she knew she wouldn't have left, until after she'd at least tried to do something to help.

When she'd gone to her father to discuss her desire to help the women and children of Syria, he'd forbidden her to go there, fearing for her life in the war-torn nation. He'd suggested she go to Africa and help the poor women and children there.

His suggestion had given her the idea of how she could leave Venice with her father's permission and blessing.

While he'd been busy running his businesses, she'd left Venice on a mission to help all right. But not the poor children in Africa. Instead, she'd gone to help the women of Syria and Iraq who'd been raped, abused and killed for no other reason than they were women, and ISIS considered them lesser beings than sheep.

The injustice of their plight had pulled Isabella out of her sheltered life.

Meeting Ronin, the American Navy SEAL, and learning about all he'd gone through during his training, left her even more convinced she should do something. She was young and strong and could learn how to defend herself and others, much like Ronin had.

Their time together during Carnival was like a dream. Before Ronin, she hadn't believed in love at first sight. But their meeting at her father's masquerade ball had been nothing short of magical. He'd swept her off her feet with his dashing pirate costume and relentless pursuit of her hand in a dance.

Her decision to leave the ball with him had been spontaneous and reckless, but she'd never regretted it, not even for a moment. Her father's bodyguards had taken the brunt of her father's ire over her escape, but she couldn't regret the time she'd spent with the American.

He'd taught her more about making love and following her dreams than she'd learned in all of her twenty-six years as Marcus Pisano's daughter.

When he'd left her in the Piazza San Marco, she'd missed Ronin terribly and had thought about following him back to the States.

However, he hadn't promised her forever with him, nor had he invited her to be with him in Virginia. Ronin had made it very clear he had an important job as a SEAL, and he took it seriously. He traveled the world in an attempt to end terrorism and help others regain control of their own countries.

Ronin's dedication to his work, and the tales the Syrian refugee had imparted, helped Isabella come to the realization she couldn't go on as the spoiled daughter of a multi-millionaire. She had to do something to help others.

From that moment forward, she'd immersed herself in the study of martial arts, not just mastering moves, but learning how to really defend herself against attack and how to take someone down who stood in the way of her goal. From Asaf, one of her father's hired bodyguards, a former Israeli soldier and mercenary, she'd learned how to use an entire armory of weapons and how to construct explosive devices out of normal household items.

She'd completed her training and scheduled a year-long trip to Africa to teach small children how to read and write. She'd sold the idea of the mission to her father on the understanding she'd be safe with Asaf and a contingent of bodyguards. And she'd promised to take along a female friend of hers from university.

From Venice, she'd flown to Uganda, spent a month there, teaching children and recording images she could send back to her father as proof she was still alive.

One starry night, she and Asaf had flown to Turkey and crossed the border into Syria. And thus, her mission began. Over the next year, she'd slipped into ISIS strongholds, freeing women and killing the men who'd horribly abused them.

On two occasions, she'd allowed herself to be captured in order to get inside and convince the girls and young women to escape with her.

The women she'd rescued called her their Angel of Mercy.

The men of ISIS learned of this Angel of Mercy and wanted her dead. So much so, they'd put a price on her head and threatened to kill anyone who harbored or aided her in her efforts to free the women.

Their threats hadn't stopped Isabella. But when their threats turned to reality, and the women who'd aided and helped her along the way were tortured and killed in public as a deterrent to others, Isabella knew she had to leave. By staying in Syria, she put more people at risk than she was helping.

With Asaf's help, she left the country in the dead of night, just like she'd entered. However, nothing ever went exactly according to plan.

The price on her head was too tempting. Spies lay in wait. They'd been ambushed. Since the price on her head was to deliver her alive, they'd no need to spare Asaf. He was killed outright.

Isabella returned fire, barely escaping with her own life. Under the cover of darkness, she'd traversed hostile territory on her own. Yes, she'd made it back to Italy. Yes, she'd found her way to her father's house in Venice and resumed the life of the daughter of an Italian tycoon. But nothing was ever the same. She wasn't the person she'd been when she'd left.

Her father never knew what she'd done. He'd never suspected she'd gone into enemy territory, rescued abducted women and killed ISIS murderers and rapists. All he'd learned upon her return, was that her body-guard had died, and he needed to assign her a new one.

Isabella spent the first couple of weeks at home, her heart hurting from losing her best friend and mentor, Asaf. She hadn't needed to go out. Servants brought her whatever she wanted.

But soon, the walls of her father's mansion closed in around her. She longed to be out in the open. All the nights she'd slept under the stars, with no light noise to pollute the heavens, made her wish she could see past the lights of Venice.

When she couldn't stand being inside anymore, she left the house and wandered the avenues, her bodyguards close beside her. Even the streets didn't feel the same. Everywhere she turned were memories of the days she'd spent with a handsome Navy SEAL, before she'd set off on her personal journey to save the world.

She would have thought two years would have dulled the longing for the stranger who'd changed her forever.

She found herself standing in front of Hotel Eden, staring at the place she'd spent several fabulous days, discovering her own sexuality with a man who'd taught her more about lovemaking than she'd known existed.

Isabella found herself wishing she could see him again. If only for a moment. Perhaps that time in her life had been nothing more than an exaggerated product of her memories and imagination.

From Hotel Eden, she moved through the streets, ducking into alleys when the bodyguards weren't paying attention. Soon, she'd lost them in the crowds of tourists already partying.

Her meandering led her to Piazza San Marco, where

she'd last seen Ronin. As soon as she entered the square, she viewed the sea of humanity, wondering why she'd bothered to venture out during Carnival. People jostled her, laughing and probably drunk. It wasn't as if she'd really believed she'd run into Ronin there. It was just memories that had led her to the square.

Ronin would be somewhere saving the world, one terrorist at a time.

Her chest tightened, and tears stung her eyes. Nothing was the same. She didn't belong in Venice. Isabella wasn't sure where she belonged. She didn't even feel like she belonged in her own skin.

She turned to exit the piazza when she saw a tall, dark-haired man, wearing a tight black T-shirt that stretched across broad shoulders. His hair was cut short, military-style.

Isabella's breath caught in her throat. Her feet carried her toward him. People crossed her path, blocking her way. She struggled to see the man in the black shirt, ducking around a woman in a bright, royal blue dress. Then she was there, and he was right in front of her, reaching for another woman and calling out, "Isabella."

Isabella's heart skipped several beats and then raced on.

The woman turned and smiled. She was old and gray-haired.

After two years, Isabella wasn't the same woman Ronin had known, but she had to know if this man was him.

"Ronin?" she called out, her voice soft, breathy, as if

she couldn't quite force air from her lungs. As he turned, she held her breath.

Joy surged into her chest and filled her heart. It was Ronin—not a stranger, not a dream.

"Isabella," he said and opened his arms.

She didn't hesitate for a second, but fell into his arms.

Finally, she'd come home.

RONIN COULDN'T BELIEVE his eyes, but the proof he held against his body convinced him he wasn't living a dream. Isabella was pressed against him, wrapping her arms around his waist.

"I never thought I'd find you," he whispered against her hair.

"I thought you were a dream," she said.

He chuckled, a happiness so pure filling him to full and overflowing. Ronin lifted her into the air and swung her around. Then he set her on the ground and kissed her like there would be no tomorrow.

She returned the kiss with a ferocity he didn't recognize. Isabella had lost weight, and her body was sinewy, her muscles tight.

When he ran his tongue along the seam of her lips, she opened to him, meeting his tongue with a warm, wet caress. She tasted of mint and coffee.

Ronin lifted his head and drank in the sight of her.

She'd cut her long wavy hair to shoulder-length. Her face was leaner and there were two new scars. One near her mouth, the other across her cheekbone.

He thumbed the one by her mouth. "This is new."

She laughed and ran her hand over his face. "And so are these." Her eyebrows dipped, and she stepped back, running her gaze over him from head to toe. "Are you all right? Have you been in some pretty bad firefights?"

Ronin shrugged. He didn't want to think about all that had happened in the past two years. "Nothing unusual." He narrowed his eyes, studying her scars. "How did you get these scars?" He brushed the scarf back from her face, and it fell onto her shoulders.

"Nothing unusual," she echoed. Isabella glanced away, fumbling with the light blue fabric, trying to pull it up over her head.

A man in a jester's costume danced by, caught the end of her scarf and spun away.

Isabella gasped and grabbed for it.

Ronin yelled, "Hey!"

The jester flung the blue wisp of fabric into the air. A breeze caught it, and it drifted to the ground.

Isabella ducked her head, her hair falling over her face as she lunged for the ground.

Ronin dropped down to his haunches, reaching the garment first.

Over their heads a loud crack could be heard, followed by the sound of rapid-fire explosions.

Isabella flatted herself to the ground.

Ronin fell on top of her, shielding her body from attack.

Women screamed, and the crowd surged toward the exits.

People tripped and fell over them. Ronin knew

they'd be trampled to death if they stayed on the ground. He hooked his arm around Isabella's waist and scooped her off the ground.

She held onto the scarf and ran alongside him.

Ronin glanced around, searching for the best way out of the piazza. As he panned the area, his gaze landed on the jumbo-tron display screen. The screen was wrecked, with gaping holes ripped through its center.

Overhead, more bursts exploded, raining confetti down on the piazza.

People stopped running and laughed. Some raised their hands to the confetti and danced around.

Ronin realized some of the blasts were confetti being launched into the air. But confetti couldn't have destroyed the jumbo-tron. Could it?

While others stopped running and resumed their celebration, Ronin hurried Isabella out of the piazza. If a confetti bomb could destroy a screen, he could only imagine what it could do if it hit a person.

Once out of the piazza, Isabella paused long enough to wrap the scarf over her hair and halfway across her face. Then she led the way through the streets.

Ronin followed, unsure of where she was taking him, but trusting that she knew where she was going. When they arrived in front of Hotel Eden, Ronin smiled. "You remembered."

Isabella didn't pause to respond. She glanced in both directions, and then dove for the door.

Once inside, she spoke in rapid Italian to the clerk at the small desk tucked into a corner. The young clerk shook his head. She spoke again, and the clerk raised his hands, palms up.

Isabella sighed. "They have no rooms available."

Ronin's lips twitched upward on the corners. "Let me try." He turned to the clerk. *"Prenotazione per Magnus."*

The clerk looked down at his computer screen, a frown pulling his eyebrows together. "Ronin Magnus?" He glanced up.

Ronin smiled. *"Sì."*

Isabella's lips twisted into a wry grin. "This is Carnival. Rooms are impossible to find. You had to have made that reservation months ago."

He shrugged. "I did. I knew I'd be in Ireland for my brother's wedding, so I scheduled more leave after the wedding and booked my hotel here in Venice."

She tilted her head. "Why?"

Before he could answer, the clerk handed him a key and gave him the room number.

The old hotel had no elevator, and his room was on the third floor. He led the way up the narrow, wooden staircase, knowing this structure wouldn't pass building codes in the US. At the top of the stairs were three doors, none of which were the number on the key tag he held in his hand.

Having been there two years ago, Ronin knew to go through the middle door, which led into a hallway with three more doors and a floor-to-ceiling mirror at the end of the hallway.

Isabella chuckled behind him. "You got the same room?"

He nodded. "I asked for it, specifically." Then he pushed the mirror, and it folded like an accordion, revealing yet three more doors. The last door on the right was his destination. He pressed the key into the lock.

Isabella covered his hand with hers. "Why did you come here?"

He turned to her, gripped her arms and stared down into her eyes. "I came to find you."

CHAPTER 3

Isabella's heart leaped into her throat, and her eyes stung. As she'd walked through the streets of Venice, she'd known in the back of her mind she'd been looking for Ronin. More than anything, she wanted to recapture what she'd felt when she'd been in his arms.

After all she'd gone through, all the training, the rescues, being captured, and then losing her mentor, Isabella knew she couldn't go back to being the person she'd once been. Nor did she want to.

But she didn't feel comfortable in her old home, living with her father, being under constant guard and worrying about potential kidnappers. More than that, she worried she might have brought her own hell back from Syria.

With a price on her head, she might bring chaos to her father's house. Just because she'd made it out of Syria didn't mean ISIS would give up looking for her. She'd rescued many women, killed many ISIS rebels, and had even been responsible for the death of Haji, the brother of Abu Ahmad al-Jahashi, an influential ISIS leader.

Abu Ahmad had sworn his vengeance on her. It would be only a matter of time before they found her.

She couldn't be certain, but the explosion in the piazza, before the confetti bombs, might have been someone aiming for her. The burst had occurred at the same time she'd made a dive for her scarf.

Then again, it could have been a coincidence. But the one thing Isabella had learned during her year as the Angel of Mercy was that coincidences didn't exist. All things happened for a reason.

Now, tucked away in Hotel Eden, with the man who'd made her feel so much more than any man she'd ever known in her twenty-eight years, she felt safe. He had his life and she had hers, but for this brief moment, they were the center of each other's universes and nothing, or no one, would come between them.

No sooner had Ronin closed and locked the door behind him then Isabella fell into his arms, as if no time had passed since last they were together. Everything about being in his arms felt right.

He tipped her head and kissed her forehead, her eyelids and, finally, her lips. "You've haunted me ever since I left Venice two years ago."

She shook her head. "Not a night passed that I didn't think of you." And it was true. In the darkest days of desperation, her heart turned to the most magical time of her life. The days she'd spent with Ronin in this hotel, making love through the night until the sun shone high in the Italian sky each day. "I missed you the moment you left."

"And I couldn't stop thinking about you, no matter where in the world I was."

Isabella sighed and pressed her forehead to his chest. "We swore no strings. No commitments."

He tipped her chin upward. "What if I want strings?" he whispered and brushed her lips with his.

Isabella's heart fluttered and sped ahead. What was he saying? Dared she dream of another future? She shook her head. "We are from two different worlds."

"No, Isabella." He brushed his thumb across the scar beside her mouth. "We are from the same world."

Again, she rested her forehead against his chest. "There is much you do not know about me." She was a danger to others. Even coming home to Venice brought danger to her family. How could she consider being with this man when he had his own job to do, his own life to lead? "No strings, Ronin. That's why we parted before. It has to be that way."

"Why?"

She took one step backward and placed her hands on his chest. "It has to be that way. I cannot explain. If you cannot accept this, I must leave now. I will not prolong the pain."

His hands clamped around her arms, and he dragged her against him. "Don't go. I just found you, again. I can't let you go so soon."

Isabella curled her fingers into his shirt. "Promise me...when it comes time for me to leave, you will let me go and forget about me?"

He shook his head. "I can't make that promise. I will never forget you."

"At least, promise you will let me go."

Ronin drew in a deep breath and let it out slowly. "I promise to let you go, if that is truly what you want."

She narrowed her eyes and stared up into his. Finally, she nodded and melted against him, slipping her arms around his waist. "For now, I only want to hold you."

"I want so much more." When she opened her mouth to protest, he pressed a finger to her lips. "But I'll take whatever time you will give me. For now."

Isabella kissed his finger and slipped her arms around him. "Then hold me. Love me, and let me love you in return." She gripped his shirt and tugged it free of his waistband, a smile spreading across her face.

He pulled the scarf from her head and tossed it to the corner. He unbuttoned her shirt and pushed it from her shoulders, letting it fall to the floor at her feet.

With her hand on the button of his jeans, she pushed the rivet through the hole and slowly unzipped. His cock sprang free, long and stiff. She palmed it, caressing the length between her fingers.

Ronin sucked in a deep breath, rolled his head back and closed his eyes. "You make me so hard."

"You make me so hot," she whispered.

The rest of her clothing flew off as Ronin backed her toward the narrow bed. When the backs of her knees bumped against the mattress, she stopped.

Ronin took a step backward, holding her at arm's length, his gaze sweeping over her naked body, caressing her with his eyes. "I don't know how you do it, but you're even more beautiful than before."

Heat filled her cheeks, and she returned his perusal with a survey of her own, her glance running his length. "How do you keep in such amazing shape? I swear your shoulders are even broader."

"The better carry you to bed, my dear." He waggled his eyebrows and scooped her up into his arms. He kissed her soundly and laid her across the bed, draping her legs over the side. Then he stepped between them, nudging her thighs apart with his knees.

With her heart thundering against her ribs, Isabella pushed up on her elbows and widened her legs, allowing Ronin to move closer to her damp entrance.

"Remember the last time we made love?" he asked.

Isabella's breath caught, and her core tightened. She nodded. "I remember."

"Then we'll begin at the end." He dropped to his knees, parted her thighs and bent to take her with his mouth.

RONIN COULDN'T RECALL EVER BEING as hard as he was. He wanted to skip the foreplay and drive deep into Isabella, but he was determined to remind her how good they were together. And he loved making her come, loved hearing the sound of her cries. Isabella went all-in when making love. Ronin loved that about her.

He started slowly, parting her folds with his thumbs.

Isabella's hands flattened on top of the comforter.

Ronin blew a warm stream of air across her clit.

She inhaled sharply. "Stop."

"Stop?" He let go of her folds and raised his head. "Really? You want me to stop?"

"No, that's not what I meant." She drew in a shaky breath. "Stop teasing me."

Ronin chuckled and repositioned his thumbs against her soft folds, pulling them back to expose the sliver of flesh packed with nerves. "Perhaps this will be better," he suggested. Then he touched the tip of his tongue to her there, sliding it along the length of her nubbin.

Isabella's fingers curled into the comforter, and her hips rose to push herself closer to him. "Oh, my. *Yessss.*"

"Like that?"

"Mmm," she murmured. "Again, please."

He obliged, taking his time, laving her clit with long, sensuous strokes.

Her back arched off the mattress.

Changing tactics, he flicked his tongue against her and sucked the nubbin into his mouth, pulling gently.

She muttered something in Italian and transferred her hands from the comforter to his hair, weaving her fingers between the strands. "Don't stop."

"Oh, honey, I hadn't planned on stopping. I want you hot and wet when I come inside you."

"Do it. Do it, now," she begged.

"Not yet. You're not quite there yet."

"Oh, but I am."

He slid a finger into her channel and swirled it around.

Isabella moaned. She was so wet. So ready.

But not there yet.

Determined to bring her to the brink, Ronin slid another finger inside and caressed her clit with his tongue, sliding in and out, over and over.

Isabella arched her back off the bed, her cries growing louder. *"Por favore. Pleeeaaasssee."*

He intensified his efforts until her body stiffened and her fingers dug into his scalp. One more flick of his tongue, and she gasped.

Her body shook with the force of her release. Her breath caught and held, her muscles spasming for a long time. Finally, she collapsed against the mattress and drew in a deep, shaky breath. She rested for only a moment before she grasped his arms and urged him up onto the bed. Up onto her.

"Now," she said. "Make love to me."

He leaned over her, his lips a breath away from hers. "Miss me?"

"Si." She lifted her head, just enough to seal their lips, and then said into his mouth, "More than you can imagine."

Ronin scooted her up on the bed and parted her thighs with a nudge of his knee. Then he positioned his cock at her opening and paused. Sucking in a deep breath, he let it go. "Damn. I almost forgot."

"What?" She gripped his hips and urged him to enter her. "What did you forget?"

"Protection."

Her eyes rounded. *"Madre de Dio.* How could I forget?" She shook her head.

"Not to worry. I have some in my wallet." He rolled

off the bed, grabbed for his jeans and dug into his wallet. When his fingers wrapped around the foil packet, he held it up.

"*Grazie.*" Isabella reached for the packet, tore it open and sat up to apply the condom to his thick shaft.

Ronin liked the feel of her hands on him, the way they deftly smoothed the protection over the tip and down his length.

At the base of his shaft, she paused to cup his balls. "I've missed you," she said. Then she scooted back on the bed and opened herself to him.

By that time, Ronin could barely breathe. He couldn't believe his luck in finding her the first time. But to find her again was beyond luck. It was a miracle. He settled between her legs and touched his cock to her entrance. "Slow and easy? Or hard and fast?"

She gripped his hips and stared up into his face. "Hard and fast. I want you now."

He drove into her, his shaft buried deep, surrounded by her tight channel.

Isabella dug her heels into the mattress and raised up her hips to meet him, thrust for thrust.

Hard and fast, he pumped in and out of her, shaking the bed with every move. His muscles tightened as he neared the peak and shot over the top. Dropping down on her, he held her close, his shaft throbbing inside her.

She wrapped her arms around him and held on.

He had to be crushing the breath out of her, but she refused to let him go.

Finally, she loosened her hold.

Ronin rolled to his side, taking her with him and

cradling her against his body. For a long time he lay, bathed in perspiration and the afterglow of the best sex he'd ever experienced. Only, to him, what they'd just done was more than sex. Together, they made music. As dumb as that sounded in his own thoughts, it was what it was. Music. Making love with Isabella was a symphony of muscles, nerves and movement that sang to the deepest part of Ronin's heart. He didn't want the music to ever stop.

He turned to her, kissed her forehead and then her lips. "What are we going to do? I can't let you go again."

She opened her mouth to speak.

Pounding on the door jerked them both upright.

CHAPTER 4

Isabella yanked the edge of the sheet to her chest and leaped out of the bed. She immediately headed for the window.

Ronin pulled on his jeans and headed for the door.

"What are you doing?" Isabella demanded in a sharp whisper.

"Someone knocked on the door." He stared across the room at her, his brows furrowed. "It might be the desk clerk with further instructions."

"Don't answer," she dropped the sheet and grabbed for her clothes, pulling the shirt over her head and dragging her trousers up over her hips.

"Who else would it be, besides the clerk?" Ronin shook his head and turned toward the door.

"Please," Isabella said. "You never know. It could be someone who wants to hurt us." She jammed her feet into her shoes, her heart racing. Her gut was telling her they had to get out of there. She threw open the window and leaned out, only to curse in Italian. The third-story window had a three-story drop to the murky canal below.

RONIN GRIPPED her arms from behind. "You can't be serious. Jumping into the canal from this high up can get you killed. You don't know what's beneath the surface of the water."

"We can't stay."

Pounding sounded on the door again, and someone shouted in Italian, "*Apri la porta!*"

"What is he saying?" Ronin asked.

"Open the door." Isabella scooped the sheet from the floor and tied the end to the bedframe near the window. Then she yanked the bottom sheet off the mattress and tied it to the sheet tied to the bed.

"What are you doing?" he asked again, raking a hand through his hair. His dark brow furrowed.

"We have to get out of here," she insisted. "Before they break down the door."

"Why would they break down the door?"

"To get to us. To hurt us." She shied away from saying *me*. The people after her wouldn't hesitate to hurt or kill anyone with her, so it wasn't just about her life. Ronin's life was equally in danger.

The pounding stopped. For a moment, Isabella thought perhaps that whoever had been at the door had gone away. But for how long and how far? Were they on the other side, waiting for them to emerge?

Then a loud bang on the door sounded, and the frame split but held.

"We have to leave," she whispered furiously. "Now. Before someone gets hurt."

Ronin's gaze locked with hers. His expression hardening. "Who would want to hurt us?"

She shook her head. "No time to explain. Just go." Isabella took his hand and laid the sheet in it. "You go first."

Ronin glanced out the window and frowned. "If you're so certain someone is trying to hurt us, *you* should go first."

"Please," she begged. "Go."

Another loud crash sounded at the door, and it slammed open.

Isabella shoved Ronin toward the window and planted herself between the two men rushing into the room, and the man behind her.

"*Tu chi sei?*" she demanded.

Neither man spoke. Instead, they started to push past her.

No. They couldn't hurt Ronin.

Dropping into a ready stance, Isabella waited for the right moment, and then sprang. She caught one of the men by surprise, knocking him into the other guy.

Both men slammed to the floor, one on top of the other. While they struggled to untangle themselves from each other, Isabella turned to Ronin. "Jump," she said.

Ronin pushed the sheet into her hands. "Ladies, first," he bit out.

"No, you—"

Before Isabella could finish her sentence, Ronin grabbed her around her waist and swung her over the window ledge. "Hold on tight."

Isabella grabbed the sheet and glanced up at the rugged SEAL. "But what about you?"

"I'm right behind you." He turned just as one of their attackers launched himself toward them, and threw a punch that connected with the side of his face. "Now, go!" he shouted over his shoulder.

Isabella shimmied down the makeshift rope of sheets to the canal below. When she ran out of sheet, she let herself drop into the water. It was over her head and she went under. She surfaced and glanced up at the window three stories over her head.

Ronin had yet to climb out the window. What was taking him so long?

An unfamiliar face leaned out the window, holding the sheets in his hand. He let go and the sheet drifted down to the water. Then he disappeared back into the room above.

Isabella kicked hard, propelling herself toward an opening in the wall. She dragged her body up onto a landing and ran through an alley, emerging in front of Hotel Eden in time to run into her two bodyguards.

In Italian she said, "Hurry, follow me." She burst through the door in time to find the other two attackers hauling Ronin down the stairs, unconscious.

Her heart leaped into her throat, and she shot forward, ready to take on the men who'd hurt her love.

She didn't get far. The bodyguards behind her snagged her arms and held her back.

In Italian, she demanded, "What are you doing? Let go of me."

The big one named Lorenzo responded. "They are protecting you from this man."

"What?" Isabella stopped struggling. It wasn't getting her anywhere, and she had to clear up this mess. "The man is unconscious. They hurt him. How is he a threat to me?" She glared at the two men holding Ronin. "That man is with me. Unhand him, at once!" she demanded. "I order you to let him go."

The men shook their heads as one.

"They cannot." Lorenzo interjected. "They are following your father's orders."

"This is ridiculous." She shook free of Lorenzo's grip and glared at Matteo, the other man holding her arm, until he released her, too. "I'll have words with my father."

Lorenzo nodded.

Isabella crossed to Ronin and cupped his face. A goose-egg-sized knot was forming on his forehead. She touched it gently, and he moaned.

His eyes fluttered open for a moment. When he saw her standing in front of him, he closed them again.

She swallowed hard to dislodge the lump forming in her throat, praying his injuries weren't life-threatening. "What are you going to do with this man?"

"We're taking him to your father." Lorenzo jerked his head to the side.

The two men holding Ronin up carried him through

the cramped lobby and out the door to the street beyond.

Isabella hurried to keep up with them.

They didn't stop until they reached a portal to the canal.

When they looked like they would drop Ronin into the boat, Isabella cried out, "Wait."

She climbed down into the boat and held out her arms. "Okay, you can ease him into the boat."

They lowered Ronin until his feet touched the bottom of the little boat.

Isabella hooked her arm around his waist and tried to absorb his weight as the two big men released him.

She held him up for a moment, but he was still unconscious and a deadweight against her. She sat down hard on a padded seat and tried her best to keep him from banging his head again on something hard.

The four bodyguards climbed into the boat. Lorenzo took the helm and guided the craft through the canals to her father's palatial mansion.

Her heart beating hard in her chest, Isabella braced herself for the upcoming confrontation with her strong-willed father. She wondered how many of her secrets she would have to reveal in order to save Ronin from further injury.

She inhaled a deep breath and followed the two big men carrying Ronin into the building. They carried him into her father's study and deposited him onto a leather couch.

Isabella dropped to her knees beside him and touched her fingers to the base of his neck, searching for a pulse. Her breath held until she felt the strong, steady beat beneath her fingertips.

Andre, the butler, entered a moment later, carrying a tray with an assortment of tea things, including a pot and several teacups.

"Andre, call for the doctor," Isabella commanded. "Tell him it's urgent."

"I'll be the judge of that," came a booming voice from the foyer. Her father, a big man with an even bigger personality, entered the room.

Marcus Pisano was a self-made multi-millionaire who'd clawed his way to the top of the shipping and import-export business. He'd started out as a poor boy from the one of the dirtiest neighborhoods of Rome and worked his way up. Known as a shrewd and ruthless businessman, he didn't suffer fools, nor did he hesitate to call them out.

Ronin moaned and opened his eyes. When he saw Isabella and the four men standing behind her, he pushed up on his elbows. "Isabella, run," he said, his voice husky. He swayed and would have fallen back if Isabella hadn't been there to steady him.

"It's okay," she said softly. "They aren't going to hurt you."

"I'm not worried about me," he said, scrubbing a hand down his face. "I'm worried about you."

"They won't hurt me." She pursed her lips and glared at Marcus Pisano. "They work for my father."

Ronin leaned forward, over his knees and buried his face in his hands. He winced with his fingers bumped against the knot on his forehead. "Your father? I don't understand."

"Let me explain," Isabella's father said in English. "You were found with my daughter. My bodyguards assumed you'd kidnapped her. They subdued you and brought you here. Give me one reason why I shouldn't turn you over to the police and have you arrested for assault and wrongful imprisonment?"

"You can't have him arrested." Isabella leaped to her feet and placed herself between Ronin and her father. "This man is my fiancé."

RONIN SHOOK HIS HEAD, trying to make sense of what was going on. He started to open his mouth and protest Isabella's words, but it was exactly what he'd wanted from her. He might not have known what he'd hoped to gain out of coming to Venice when he'd set out to find Isabella, but after seeing her and making love to her like no time had passed between them, he knew. He wanted her in his life forever.

But she'd been the one insisting on no strings, no commitment. Then why was she announcing their engagement to her father? Hell, Ronin hadn't even asked her to marry him yet.

And why the hell did his head hurt so fucking bad?

Then he remembered. While he'd been punching one of the goons who'd stormed their room at Hotel Eden, the other had stepped up beside him with a chair and hit him in the head with it.

Ronin touched the knot and winced.

Fiancé.

Funny, but he'd never expected to hear that word in relation to himself. For that matter, he'd never expected his brother Wyatt to marry, or his other brother Mack to get engaged. They were career military men, each in their chosen branch and following a path they'd entered upon completion of high school.

From a family legacy of military men, Ronin knew the hardships military families lived with when the soldier, sailor, airman or Marine was deployed. Hell, he'd seen his mother and father struggle to keep their shit together when they were separated for six months to a year and a half at a time. He didn't wish that on any woman. His mother had been strong, but she'd had moments when she'd cried her heart out, wondering if her husband would return home alive or in a body bag.

Ronin had sworn he'd never marry, just to avoid that kind of heartache. But he hadn't met Isabella when he'd made that promise to himself. After two years of wondering what had happened to the woman he'd found in Venice, all the nights thinking about her, wishing she was lying beside him, he couldn't stay away a moment longer.

Now that he had found her, he couldn't imagine letting her go again. But was it right for him to suggest a life with him? Hell, it didn't matter at the moment, she'd just announced their engagement to her father. Perhaps she'd changed her mind and wanted to be with him, no matter the cost.

He could always hope, and do his best to make her happy when they were together.

When his head stopped spinning, he looked up, capturing Isabella's gaze first. She reached out her hand.

He grabbed it and held on, pushing to his feet. His vision blurred, but he blinked hard, forcing back the gray clouds until he could see straight and stand without swaying. Finally, he faced the man who stood as tall as he in a black, pinstripe business suit, sporting a red tie. He was barrel-chested with olive-toned skin, and black-haired with bold streaks of gray. The man was an imposing figure. But he didn't scare Ronin.

Ronin slipped one hand around Isabella's waist and held out his other hand to the man he assumed was her father. "Mr. Pisano, Ronin Magnus."

Isabella's father narrowed his eyes and stared into Ronin's face without taking his hand.

After a moment, Ronin dropped his outstretched arm and squared his shoulders. "I would have first asked you for Isabella's hand in marriage, but it all happened so fast, I didn't have time." Which was true. And he hadn't thought she'd say yes. But her father didn't have to know that.

"As far as I'm concerned, there is no engagement." Her father lifted his chin and stared down his nose at Ronin. "You're American, no?"

Ronin nodded. "Yes, sir."

Mr. Pisano snorted. "Americans are loud, arrogant and annoying."

"I'm sorry you feel that way."

"It doesn't matter how he feels about Americans," Isabella said. "I love this man and intend to marry him."

Hearing her defense of him made Ronin's heart swell.

"You cannot have known him long enough to know your heart," her father said.

"I've known him for two years."

"How can that be?" Her father shook his head. "You've been gone for the past year."

"We met two years ago," Ronin answered. "Here. In Venice."

Mr. Pisano stared at Ronin suspiciously. "This is the first I've heard of you."

The man had a point. If Ronin were in his shoes, he'd be just as hesitant to believe the story they were telling.

"We met two years ago and fell in love. But I'm a military man. I've been deployed. It wasn't until yesterday I could return to find my Isabella," Ronin pulled her closer to his side. "I came to find the woman I couldn't get out of my mind or heart."

Pisano snorted. "Two years is a long time. Too long. I will not agree with this union." He jerked his head toward one of the bodyguards. "Show him out of my home."

A big guy with dark eyes and coal-black hair advanced on him.

Isabella stepped between them and held up her hand. "No. If you throw out Ronin, I'm going with him."

"You'll stay where you belong," Pisano said.

"I belong with my fiancé," she shot back at him. "I go where he goes."

For a long moment, the father and daughter glared at each other.

Ronin fought the urge to laugh. They looked so much alike in their stubborn stances.

Finally, Mr. Pisano sighed. "Very well. He will stay with us, here. I'm a firm believer in keeping your enemy close." With that final word, the elder Pisano spun and left the room.

Three of the bodyguards followed, leaving the big guy with the black hair.

In perfect English, he said, "Your father is only trying to protect you. There have been attempts on his life. He does not wish for you to be hurt. When you leave his home, please, don't try to leave without me and the other bodyguards assigned."

Isabella raised her chin, much like her father had. "I'll do as I please."

Lorenzo nodded. "You make our duties more difficult. But we will prevail."

Lorenzo left Isabella and Ronin alone.

Ronin waited until he knew no one could overhear their conversation before he pulled Isabella into his arms. "What was that all about?'

"I had to say it."

"That you are my fiancé?" He smoothed damp hair out of her face. "Why?"

Her gaze shot to the corner of the room. "I knew if I didn't, my father might have had you arrested or worse."

"Worse?"

"Some of my father's enemies have...how shall I say...disappeared." She looked up at him, her eyebrows meeting at the center of her forehead. "I couldn't let anything happen to you."

"So, you lied to your father to save my ass." Ronin shook his head. "Not that I'm complaining. I only wish you were my fiancé."

She laid a hand on his chest. "You know it cannot be. I can't bring you into my life. I have too many secrets that could destroy us both."

He gripped her arms and forced her to look him square in the eye. "What secrets?"

"Secrets not even my father knows," she whispered.

"Then tell me. I need to know what I'm up against."

She reached up to touch the lump on his forehead, stopping short. "You've already been hurt because of me. We need to stage a breakup and you can go back home. Come. We can do it now." She grabbed his hand and pulled him toward the foyer.

Ronin dug his heels in, refusing to fall in with her plan. She was afraid of something, and he'd be damned if he left now without knowing what that something was. "I'm not going anywhere. I'm in Venice for two weeks. I'm not leaving until I'm good and ready. Preferably with you." He clamped his arm around her waist and crushed her body against his. "I didn't come all this way to be scared away."

"But you don't understand. My life is…complicated."

"And mine isn't?" He chuckled. "Kiss me and tell me you want me to leave."

Her eyes widened and she shook her head. "No."

He lowered his head until their mouths were so close he could taste her breath. "Kiss me," he whispered.

She stiffened, her hands on his chest as if to push him away. Instead, her fingers curled into his shirt, and she dragged him closer. Isabella rose on her toes and pressed her lips to his, thrusting her tongue past his teeth to caress his in a long, sweeping motion that left him in little doubt of her attraction to him.

He took her offering and gave back, thrusting and tangling his tongue with hers until they were both breathless.

The sound of someone clearing his throat interrupted their moment.

Isabella ducked her head and moved back a step.

Ronin let one hand drop to the side, resting the other at the small of her back when they both turned to face the young man wearing a similar suit to the one Mr. Pisano had worn.

"Am I interrupting?" he asked, his English perfect with just a hint of an Italian accent.

"Oh, Niccolo, we were just leaving Father's study." Isabella waved a hand toward the man. "This is Niccolo Costa, my father's assistant. Niccolo, this is Ronin Magnus...my fiancé. Niccolo is the son of one of Father's oldest friends. He's working as Father's assistant to learn the business. He hopes one day to run one of his own."

For a split second, Costa's eyes narrowed, and his lips tightened.

If Ronin hadn't been watching him closely, he might not have caught the nuance because, in the next moment, Niccolo smiled and held out his hand.

Ronin took the man's hand and almost dropped it.

The man's grip was weak and cold. He shook his hand with his usual strong grasp and let go.

Niccolo clasped both of his hands together, rubbing the one Ronin had shaken as if nursing a wound. "What a surprise. I didn't know Isabella was dating. I didn't realize she'd been out of the house for the past two weeks since she'd returned home."

"It's a long story," Isabella said. She took Ronin's hand and led him toward the door. "Right now, I'd like a shower and fresh clothes."

"Perhaps you could tell me the story sometime. And also, why are you all wet?"

"Perhaps I would, if it were any of your business," Isabella muttered under her breath as she dragged Ronin from the room and up a winding staircase he seemed to recognize.

Ronin stopped halfway up and frowned. "Isn't this the place where I met you?"

He could picture her in her bandit costume, standing on the landing above, her hands on her hips, her eyes alight with daring and challenge.

"Your father is the man who hosted the masquerade ball?"

She nodded and continued up the stairs, urging him to follow. "Yes."

"I understood the man who sponsored the annual ball was a billionaire shipping tycoon."

She nodded. "Yes. That would be my father."

"Holy hell." As he put it together, Ronin pulled free of her hand and stood still on the stairs. "Pisano." He said the name, rolling it around on his tongue. "Marcus

Pisano?" He stared up at Isabella. "*The* Marcus Pisano who had an entire spread about him in that tabloid magazine? The self-made millionaire?"

Isabella sighed. "Billionaire. So, he's my father. I am not my father."

No, she wasn't. But she was the daughter of a billionaire. Hell, way out of his league. What the hell could he offer her that she didn't already have?

Nothing.

CHAPTER 5

ISABELLA'S HEART slipped into her belly as she saw the shock and anger slip across Ronin's face.

"Oh, do what you like. I'm tired, wet and I want a shower. I don't feel like answering questions about my father. Marcus Pisano is my father. I am his daughter. But that's not all I am. I am a woman in charge of my own destiny. And right now, my immediate future includes a shower. Come along, or stay here. I don't care." She turned and marched up the stairs and into the bedroom that had been hers for most of her life.

Footsteps sounded behind her.

She would have smiled, but her heart hurt. Even Ronin had been affected by the knowledge she was the daughter of a very wealthy man.

Well, what had she expected? All her life, she'd been judged based on her father's wealth. Everything about her had been made public until she'd disappeared into what everyone assumed was the wilds of Africa.

In Syria, she had been the Angel of Mercy, not the daughter of a wealthy man. She'd made differences in lives, not fashion. No one cared what designer dress she wore or what gala she attended. She was the gun-toting woman on a mission to save other women from fates worse than their own deaths.

And she had made a difference.

Isabella grabbed clean panties and a dress from her closet and entered the bathroom, slamming the door behind her. Let Ronin think what he liked. She wasn't her father. She could make it on her own. Hell, she'd fought her way out of enough tight situations she'd proven to herself she could survive without her father's money and status.

The only reason she'd come back to Venice was the simple fact she loved her father, despite his overbearing attitude toward her. And Venice held memories she wasn't ready to leave behind. Namely, her memories of Ronin and their time together during Carnival.

Yet, that time had been a masquerade. Ronin hadn't known who she was. She could have been any guest at her father's ball. He'd treated her like a woman, not a rich debutante. That was part of the reason he'd captured her attention and held it for so long. That and his incredible body packed tightly with muscles, and the way he made her come alive when he made love to her. She also loved his chuckle that seemed to come from deep inside him. The man had a sense of humor, despite what he'd witnessed in war.

When Isabella had returned to Venice, she'd needed a lighter look on life. After a year in Syria, fighting for women who didn't know a better life, she'd seen some of the worst of human nature. Her heart was heavy with the loss of those she couldn't help and those she'd left behind to defend themselves.

Seeing Ronin in Piazza San Marco had been an uplifting breath of freedom and fresh air all wrapped up in one strong man's presence.

Now, he stood on the other side of that door, grappling with the fact she was a tycoon's daughter. Would he walk away because she'd kept that little secret from him? Or would he want more of what her father could give him?

Isabella shook her head. She couldn't imagine Ronin wanting to profit off her association with her father. No, he wasn't that kind of guy. He fought the good fight for what was right. He wasn't a gun for hire, and he wouldn't be lured by money to do something against his code of ethics.

At least, that's the Ronin Isabella remembered. Two years could change a person. She knew, because her time in Syria had changed her. For the better, she hoped.

Isabella peeled the damp clothing from her body and stepped into the large, spa-like shower surrounded by glass tile and white marble. She turned on the water and stepped underneath the spray before it warmed, loving the cool water washing across her warm skin. In the desert, she'd gone days, sometimes weeks without a shower. When possible, she'd bathed in streams in the dead of night to avoid detection by the enemy. The water had been frigid, but welcome as it was now.

Perhaps the cold temperature would chase away the heat she'd felt at Ronin's touch.

She lifted her face to the spray, letting the little drops pummel her face and wash away the stench of the canal water. When the water warmed, she reached for the shampoo only to run into a thick, muscular arm.

Isabella spun, ready to fight only to find Ronin standing naked in the shower with her.

"Tell me to leave and I will. But I'd rather stay." He lathered a handful of shampoo between his palms. "Your choice."

She drew in a deep breath.

His gaze never left hers, though she stood before him as naked as they'd been only an hour before.

She sighed and nodded. "Stay." Then she turned away from him and let him apply the shampoo to her hair.

He rubbed the suds into her scalp and massaged her head with firm, yet gentle strokes. Once he'd finished her hair, he moved his hands over her shoulders and down her arms.

The tension of the fight and flight from the bodyguards melted from her body and sluiced down the drain to be replaced by a different tension. One that built at her core and fanned out to the rest of her body in a heat that flowed to her very fingertips.

Ronin slipped his hands around her waist and pulled her close to his body. His cock nudged her bottom.

"Do you know what you do to me?" she whispered.

"Sweetheart, it can't be half of what you do to me."

His hands came up to cup her breasts, his fingers tweaking the tips of her nipples.

Isabella moaned and leaned against him. "Why can't I resist you?"

He kissed the side of her neck, just below her ear. "Why would you want to?"

"I'm a woman who likes control over her life."

"And I make you lose that control?" He chuckled. "That's the best compliment I've ever heard."

"Don't you understand?" Isabella turned in his arms and cupped his cheeks between her hands. "I don't want to be dependent on any man for anything." She stared into his eyes, her heart beating so fast it made her dizzy. "Ever."

"Darlin', I don't want a woman dependent on me for anything. I need a strong woman who can stand on her own, especially when I'm not around. Because, face it, I'm not around a lot. My gig with the Navy takes me away more than I'm home."

She frowned as his words sucked away some of her internal argument. "I know that."

"My buddies who married women who depended on them are all divorced. Those women needed men who came home every night. I'm not one of those men. That's why I'm so attracted to you. You don't *need* me."

"But I *want* you." She wanted him in a way that scared her more than an ISIS fighter with a machine gun pointed at her face. She wanted him to come back to her when he wasn't out fighting the bad guys. She wanted him to make her forget all the horrors she'd seen in the desert. She wanted him to hold her, love her and make her remember what they had together.

"And I want you," he said, pressing his lips to her forehead. "Not just for great sex—because, Bella, the sex is great—but because I can see in you a woman who knows her mind and isn't afraid to use it."

Isabella laughed, the sound choking on a sudden sob. "I want you so much, but I can't do this." Even if she hadn't gone to Syria and incurred the wrath of a powerful ISIS leader, she still had the stigma of being a billionaire's daughter. Wherever she went, she'd be hounded by media and opportunists looking for a way to make money off of her. If it wasn't asking for her father to donate to their causes, they might take the less savory route of kidnapping her and holding her for ransom.

Ronin would just be a person standing in the way of those kinds of people getting to her. He'd be expendable. They'd kill him without batting an eyelash.

She pushed against his chest until she could look up at him.

Water droplets clung to his tanned face, making him even more handsome and irresistible.

"We can't be together. My life is far too complicated, and it would put you in too much danger."

His bark of laughter made her frown.

"Bella, I live for danger. It's what I do."

She shook her head. "Your kind of danger usually has a known enemy associated with it. The kind I'm talking about could be anyone walking down the streets of Venice, or New York City or anywhere else in the world. I never know who will try to grab me. My father has so much money, I've been pretty much imprisoned in this house since the day I was born. I get out on occasion, but usually accompanied by half a dozen bodyguards."

"What about today?"

She smiled and shook her head. "I escaped from my babysitters and made a run for it." Isabella waved a hand. "But they found me. And I'm lucky they did. If I hadn't run into you, someone else would have kidnapped me and held me for ransom. Since my return to Venice, my father insisted I be injected with a GPS tracking device. He doesn't want to lose me ever again."

Ronin gripped her arms. "What do you mean? Where did you come back from?"

She glanced away. Now was the time to be frank and tell him the truth. If not for her own sake then to keep him safe from potential hitmen intent on collecting the bounty on her head.

Isabella took a deep breath and let it out slowly. "I'm going to tell you something, but you can't let my father know. He won't like it and will forbid me to ever leave this house again."

"Isn't that where you are with him now?"

She shrugged. "He'll let me out with bodyguards, but I mean it. You have to promise."

Ronin held up a hand as if making a pledge in court. "I promise."

She stared at him for a moment, and then leaned close in case listening devices had been installed in her bathroom since she'd been gone. One never knew, and it didn't hurt to be cautious in this situation.

"Have you heard of the Angel of Mercy?" she whispered into his ear.

He frowned. "Maybe," he hedged. "Tell me more." His hands rested on her hips, holding her naked body close to his.

Isabella's breasts rubbed against the taut muscles of his chest, stirring feelings she didn't have time to act upon. But, oh, she wanted to. "The Angel of Mercy Abu Ahmad al-Jahashi has announced he wants captured or killed at any price?" She leaned back and waited for the recognition in Ronin's eyes to hit.

He nodded, still frowning. "Yes. So?"

Isabella jabbed her chest with her thumb. "You're looking at her."

Ronin took a moment, letting her words sink into his head. They didn't make sense. Isabella was a society princess, not a gun-toting mercenary whose mission was to free the women enslaved by ISIS.

Yes, she was strong. He could feel how sinewy her muscles were under her silky-soft skin. And her body was leaner, her beautiful face slightly weathered with fine lines showing around her mouth and eyes. And there were scars.

He ran his thumb along the scar beside her mouth and stared into her eyes.

She didn't blink. This wasn't a joke to her. Isabella was serious.

"Is that where you got this?" he asked about the scar he brushed his thumb across.

Isabella cupped his hand and leaned her cheek into his palm. "Yes. An ISIS leader backhanded me. He was wearing a ring he'd stolen off a Syrian he'd killed that day."

Ronin raised his hand to the scar on her cheek. "And this?"

Her lips thinned. "That was from a rather mean man who tried to rape me when I'd allowed myself to be captured in order to get inside the compound where they'd taken a dozen women to be used as slaves." Isabella's eyes narrowed. "I killed him."

Ronin thought he'd known this woman, but there was so much more to her than he'd given her credit for. "You're the Angel of Mercy everyone has been talking about?" he said, needing to say it out loud so he could believe.

She nodded. "I don't call myself that. The women I helped to rescue gave me that title." Her lips quirked upward. "I don't know that I deserve it." Smile fading, Isabella leaned her forehead against his chest. "When al-Jahashi put that price on my head, he also made a promise that whosoever helped me in my mission would be punished. One of the women who'd hidden me during one of my raids was found out. She was paraded naked through the streets, then raped and beheaded."

Ronin touched a finger beneath her chin and raised her face to his. Tears mingled with the water from the cooling shower spray. "You did not kill that woman. Al-Jahashi did. You couldn't save them all."

"I wanted to." She sniffed. "He killed three other women who'd had nothing to do with me. Just to show his commitment to finding me. That's when I knew I had to leave." She drew in a deep breath. "So, you see, my life is very complicated. I never know if someone will attack me to get a ransom out of my father. Or if someone will kidnap me to take me back to al-Jahashi. Or if someone will just kill me. I'm sure al-Jahashi will pay the price for my body, dead or alive." She gave him a weak smile. "Now, are you as interested in a relationship with me, knowing what a mess my life is?"

He released a breath and gave her a tight smile. "Even more so," he said, his voice husky.

"Oh, dear. That was not my intention." She laughed, the sound coming out more as a hiccup. "I was trying to scare you away."

"I told you, I'm not easily scared."

"Not even by my blustery father?"

Ronin shook his head. "The man is only trying to keep you safe." He gathered her close, reached behind her and shut off the water. Silently, he toweled her dry, squeezing the water out of her hair.

Isabella used another towel to absorb the water from his skin. By the time she worked her way down his torso, he was hard and ready for what could come next. Yet, he couldn't bring himself to make a sexual move on her. Not when she'd just told him she had a price on her head. The woman had to be nervous, jumping at shadows.

ISIS had many followers all over the world. Communication could have been spread through the computer network, and every terrorist in every country could be on the lookout for her. She might as well remain holed up in her father's mansion, surrounded by bodyguards and security cameras.

"Why did you escape your bodyguards today? Especially, knowing how dangerous that could be."

She nodded. "I needed air. I was missing my partner, Asaf, the man who'd taught me everything I needed to know before I went to Syria. He was with me through most everything until the last." Her breath caught, and she pulled her bottom lip between her teeth. "He was killed as we attempted to cross the border from Syria back into Turkey."

Ronin's chest tightened. He wrapped the towel around Isabella and tucked the end in between her breasts. "Did you love him?"

She smiled. "Yes. I did love him." Then her gaze met his. "Like a very dear, older brother." Isabella shook her head. "Are you jealous?"

He shrugged. "Yes. You spent a year or more with this man. That's long enough to fall in love."

"I spent a little over a week with you. I didn't need a year to know my feelings for you."

His gaze locked with hers. "And what are those feelings?"

She turned away, lifted a brush off the counter and dragged it through the tangles. "That I want you. That, if things were different, I could spend my life getting to know more about you. But my world is too...

"Complicated," he finished for her.

She nodded, meeting his gaze in the mirror. "I can't ask you to be a part of the chaos. This is my world. I have to live in it. You do not."

"What if I want to? What if I choose to be in your world?"

"You don't have a choice. I won't let you become a pawn in al-Jahashi's game or that of my father's enemies. Your job is hard enough without worrying about me. Can we leave it at that? I don't want to talk of a future that will never happen between me and you."

Ronin wrapped a towel around his waist and followed her into the bedroom. "Okay, for now, I'll let it slide. But I'm not done with you. Know that. You're like a tick buried beneath my skin."

"Tick?" Her eyebrows drew together. "What is this tick?"

He laughed. "A bug we have in the States that burrows into your skin and is hard to find and hard to pull out. In this case, I don't want to pull you out of my skin. I want to keep you." He pulled her into his arms and kissed her forehead. "But for now, we're engaged." Ronin held up a hand. "Only in your father's eyes."

"We need to stage a fight and a breakup. You can't be here for long, or you'll become a target just like me."

"Don't you worry about me." He bent to brush his lips across hers. "I'll take my chances."

"I really wish you wouldn't." Isabella pressed her lips to his and pushed her tongue past his teeth to toy with his. "You truly are irresistible."

"Good. Hold that thought." Then he claimed her

mouth in a kiss designed to rock her world. The longer he could hang around, the more time he had to work on her and change her resolve from sending him away to keeping him forever. In the meantime, he wanted to get a feel for the real situation. Was she in as much danger as she saw potential for? If so, how could he make her safer?

CHAPTER 6

ISABELLA WRAPPED her arms around Ronin's neck and held on tight. For all her words about breaking up and sending him away, she really didn't want him to leave.

Being in his arms made her feel safe and warm, and it was getting even warmer.

If the tent he was making with his towel was any indication, he was as hot as she was. A quick glance at the clock on her nightstand made her sigh and back away.

Ronin snagged her hand and tugged her against him. "Where are you going?"

She nodded toward the clock. "Dinner in this house is at six o'clock. My father does not like being kept waiting." Her gaze shifted to Ronin and his bare chest. Her pulse ratcheted up several notches, and her core heated to an inferno. "Then again, we have fifteen minutes..." Isabella reached for the corner of the towel tucked against her breast and released it. The towel fell to the floor.

Ronin didn't waste time. His own towel hit the ground seconds after hers. He scooped her up in his arms, wrapped her legs around his waist and backed her up against the wall.

She laughed. "Wouldn't we be more comfortable on the bed?"

"I like to be a little uncomfortable. It keeps me grounded. Fourteen minutes and counting."

"Mmm." She nibbled his ear. "Protection?"

"Damn." He carried her to the chair where he'd left his jeans and let go of her long enough to retrieve a condom from his wallet.

With her arms around his neck and her legs around his waist, Isabella held on, loving that his cock was nudging her entrance, teasing her to distraction.

Once he had the condom in hand, he tried to juggle her in his arms to get to his straining erection.

With a quick glance at the clock, Isabella made the decision. "Put me down." She unwrapped her legs from his waist, took the condom from his hands and shook her head. "We don't have time to use this. But we do have time for..." She dropped to her knees and took his full length into her hands.

He was thick, hard and throbbing. And completely magnificent in all his maleness.

Isabella touched him with the tip of her tongue, flicking all around the rim of his cock.

Ronin dug his hands into her damp hair and sucked in a deep lungful of air. "This isn't all about me."

"It is for now."

"But I want you to enjoy this."

"Believe me, I am." She drew her tongue the length of him and cupped his balls in her fingers. "I love the look on your face when you can't hold on any longer. The way you look when you let go." The she took him into her mouth. With her hands around his hips, she pulled him deeper and deeper, until he bumped against the back of her throat.

She held him there for a moment, and then pushed him out. Then slowly, she set the rhythm—in and out, in and out.

Ronin took over, moving faster, his hand on the back of her head, holding her steady as he pistoned into her mouth.

She had him where she wanted him, knew what she was doing to make him lose control and loved the rush of power it gave her.

Ronin tensed, thrust one last time and pulled free of her mouth before coming.

Isabella handed him a towel and rose to her feet, a satisfied smile stretching across her face.

"What about you?" he asked.

"I got what I wanted," she said and sailed past him into the bathroom.

A knock at the door made her pause.

"Could you answer that? I'm going to dry my hair."

"Sure. As long as it's not your bodyguards wielding a chair."

Isabella chuckled, and then leaned out the door with a frown to make sure it wasn't someone there to hurt

Ronin. When she saw Andre standing there with Ronin's bag, she left him to deal with the butler and hurried to get ready for dinner.

A minute later, Ronin appeared behind her, dressed in black slacks and a white button-down shirt. He took the hairdryer from her hands and worked on her hair while she applied makeup to her eyes. She only wore makeup to please her father. Her mother had been the perfect hostess, always dressed to perfection, her face perfectly made up. She knew how much her father missed her mother, and she knew how much she looked like her mother, Viviana. Her father never mentioned the resemblance, but the photograph he had of her, when she'd been in her twenties, could have been Isabella today.

It felt nice to have Ronin brushing her hair as it dried. He was gentle but firm, smoothing the tangles. He'd brushed her hair like that two years before, much like he was now. When her hair was straight and dry, he turned off the blower and unplugged it from the wall.

"Do you have a necktie?" she asked.

He nodded and went to the other room, returning with one in his hand. "It's been a while since I've worn one."

"Let me." She wrapped the tie around his neck and made quick work of tying a neat knot.

Before she could lower her hands, he captured her wrists.

"We're not done with the night. You know that, don't you?" he said.

She nodded. "I'm counting on it."

Then she leaned up on her toes and kissed his lips. "Two minutes left, and I have to get dressed." She let her hands trail over his chest then she grabbed the dress she'd hung on the back of the door.

"Let me," Ronin said.

"At the rate we're going, we'll never get downstairs." She handed him the dress.

He held it over her head

She slipped her arms up inside the skirt and into the straps and let the garment fall around her body.

Ronin helped smooth the dress into place and zipped the back. "Ready?"

"Just need shoes." She hurried to her closet, slipped her feet into a pair of black strappy heels and straightened. "Ready."

Ronin held out his elbow.

Isabella hooked her arm through it and led him down the stairs, through the maze of rooms on the main level to the dining room, where her father stood at the head of the table with a frown denting his brow.

"You're late," he said, he said in Italian.

Isabella released her hold on Ronin and crossed to her father to lean up and kiss his cheek. She responded in English. "But you can't be mad at me. Besides, we're only a couple minutes late. The world is still turning and you need to speak in English to make Ronin more comfortable."

In English, her father replied. "This is my house. I will be the one who is made to feel comfortable."

To Isabella's shock, Ronin addressed her father in Italian.

"You're absolutely right, Mr. Pisano. If you feel more comfortable speaking in Italian, I will manage."

Isabella shot a glance at Ronin. "I didn't know you were fluent in Italian."

He shrugged and continued in English. "I had some spare time on my hands and invested in an online course of study. I might have picked up a few words. But, seriously, if your father would prefer to speak Italian, I'll be all right."

Her father frowned. "Enough. We'll converse in English. I could use the practice." He waved to the table. "Shall we eat before our food gets cold?"

"Will Niccolo be joining us?" Isabella asked.

Her father shook his head. "He had other matters to attend. He will join us in the parlor after the meal."

Isabella nodded, her mouth forming a tight line. "Good."

Her father raised his eyebrows. "Good?"

"I like that it's only family at the table." Isabella smoothed her hands over her dress.

"If we were to have purely family at the table, Mr. Magnus would not be here," her father pointed out.

"Oh, but Ronin is practically family as my fiancé. Wouldn't you agree, Father?"

Her father frowned, giving Ronin a narrow-eyed glare.

Oh, good, Isabella thought. They'd have a nice little family meal where her father shot dirty looks at Ronin all evening. It promised to be a night of indigestion.

Isabella took the seat at her father's right. Ronin held her chair for her and waited while she sat.

When he started to sit on the other side of Isabella, her father stopped him.

"You'll sit here." Isabella's father motioned toward the place setting to his left, directly across the table from Isabella.

Ronin rounded the back of Marcus Pisano's chair and stood behind the seat indicated.

When Marcus sat, Ronin sat. Not a moment sooner.

Isabella's lips quirked upward. Her father was testing her fiancé. That he'd do it with simple table manners made Isabella nervous. What else would he judge the man on? She braced herself for a long, arduous meal. The sooner she and Ronin broke up, the better off they both would be.

Then why did she dread it? And when would be the best time to stage their little dramatic split-up scene?

RONIN DIDN'T EXPECT Isabella's father to warm to him immediately, if at all. The man had to have an instant distrust of anyone who sought to marry his daughter. As rich as he was, he had to have run interference for a multitude of would-be suitors and fortune hunters.

Mr. Pisano didn't amass a fortune by being dense. He knew most men were more interested in Isabella's potential inheritance than the woman herself.

The problem was convincing Mr. Pisano that Ronin Magnus wasn't interested in any of the billionaire's money. He only wanted to get to know his daughter better and maybe sway her to change her mind about giving him a chance at a long-term relationship.

Yeah, she had some baggage with the ISIS price tag on her head and being a prime target for a hostage and ransom attempt. But not much scared Ronin. He was up for the fight and, like every battle he entered, he entered to win.

Winning Isabella's heart was one of the most important battles he could undertake. He had no intention of losing.

A dark-haired woman carried a heavy tray into the dining room and set it on a buffet nearby. One by one, she carried soup bowls to each person at the dinner table.

"Did you and my daughter exchange correspondence while she was away in Africa?" Pisano asked.

Ronin blinked. "Africa?"

Isabella smiled brightly, though the muscles around her mouth appeared tight. "No, Father, we have not communicated for the past two years."

"Two years?" Her father shook his head. "And yet you return to Venice and immediately ask for my daughter's hand? Whatever happened to getting to know each other again before jumping into such a commitment as marriage?"

"Father, don't start on the subject of our engagement. I'd like to have a quiet meal without arguing for once."

So, the old man was argumentative and picking a fight. Ronin was always up for a good fight. Bring it. "Sir, I understand your concern. If I had a daughter as beautiful—"

"—and rich," her father added.

Ronin tipped his head in acknowledgement. "And rich, as yours, I too would be suspicious of every man walking through the door professing his love for Isabella."

Mr. Pisano's eyes narrowed. "So, you understand if I don't welcome you with open arms."

"Absolutely."

Pisano crossed his arms over his chest. "What are your intentions toward my daughter?"

"I would think it's obvious. I intend to marry your daughter."

"And will you marry her if I write her out of my will? If I give every last cent of my money to charity?"

"I would still marry your daughter. I didn't know until earlier today she was the daughter of *the* Marcus Pisano."

"Ha!" Isabella's father slammed his hand on the table. "And you immediately proposed to her."

The woman waiting on them jumped, her dark eyes rounding.

Isabella reached out to her and spoke in another language. "It's all right, Amina. My father is loud. But he is harmless."

Ronin understood her words and recognized the language. Arabic. A language with which he was all too familiar. What the hell? The woman spoke Italian, English and Arabic? What more did he not know about her?

"Since when did you learn Arabic?" her father asked.

Ronin wanted to know the answer as well.

Isabella's cheeks reddened. She focused her attention on the soup bowl in front of her. "Asaf taught me."

Her father shook his head. "A good man, Asaf. Too bad he is no longer with us. I would like to know why he left you unprotected for your trip back from Africa."

And Ronin would like to know more about the trip to Africa, which he suspected was a front for her trip to Syria, and how her father, who kept her well protected by multiple bodyguards in Italy, still didn't know she'd gone to Syria instead of Africa.

"He had good reasons," Isabella said softly.

Amina, the woman waiting on them, left the room and returned with another tray. This one full of plates of the main course, a seafood pasta with sun-dried tomatoes. The room filled with the aroma of delicious food.

Ronin's belly rumbled, but the conversation between Isabella and her father bore close scrutiny.

"Asaf worked for me," the older Pisano stated. "He should have notified me before he left you unattended."

"Father, could we not talk about Asaf?" Isabella said, her voice low and strained.

"It was very unprofessional of the man to leave you when his only job was to protect you."

Isabella slammed her palm on the table, much like her father had moments before. "Asaf couldn't do his job because he died!"

Amina almost dropped the plate she'd been carrying toward the table. She set it down quickly in front of Ronin and backed away, her eyes wide and her body trembling.

Marcus Pisano's brow furrowed. "What do you mean?"

"Asaf died protecting me." She threw down her napkin and pushed back from the table. She was on her feet and turning toward the door when her father grabbed her wrist.

"Sit, Isabella," her father commanded.

"I can't. Asaf was my friend. He died defending me. He should be alive, enjoying a long, healthy life, but he died to save me from ISIS fighters."

"I know," her father said. He stood and pulled his daughter into his arms, smoothing a hand over her dark hair. "I know now what you went through."

"You do?" She looked up at her father, tears trembling on her lashes. "How? When?"

"I sent people out to find Asaf when he didn't return with you. I learned more than I wanted to know." He shook his head. "Daughter, what you did was pure insanity. You could have been killed."

Ronin pushed back from the table and stood. "Do you want me to leave you two alone to discuss this?"

"No," Isabella responded.

"Yes," Marcus said. His gaze met Ronin's over the top of Isabella's head. "I would like a few minutes alone with my daughter. Could you wait in the study?"

Ronin nodded and left the room.

He could hear the murmur of Isabella's and her father's voices as he walked away from the father-daughter meeting. Though he would have liked to be a fly on the wall, listening to all that was said, he understood the need for Isabella to lay all her cards on the table for her father. She lived in his house; he deserved to know what he might be up against with the ISIS price on her head.

In the study, Ronin wandered around the room, looking at the mahogany book shelves lining the walls. Many of the books were in English. Some classics, some dealing with international law and a surprising collection of science fiction. The latter were newer volumes and well-read, according to the broken spines and hand-worn covers.

Footsteps sounded behind Ronin. In his peripheral vision, he noted the approach of Niccolo Costa, Pisano's executive assistant. The man wasn't armed, but he had the stance of one who had come to do battle.

"Mr. Pisano is a well-read entrepreneur," a voice came from behind him.

Ronin didn't jump or spin to face the man. He slowly replaced the book on the shelf before turning. "And apparently he likes to read fiction."

Costa shrugged. "Everyone has his faults."

"I don't see reading fiction as a fault. I myself like to pick up a book for entertainment on occasion. It helps me compartmentalize my life and remember not to take it so seriously."

"Mr. Pisano is a very serious man." The executive assistant tilted his head, looking down his nose at Ronin.

The man seemed to have a chip on his shoulder and didn't like Ronin being there.

"He didn't build an empire by playing at business."

"No, I'm sure he's focused when he needs to be."

Costa crossed his arms over his chest, all pretense of civility gone. "Why are you here?"

"You heard Miss Pisano. I'm her fiancé. I was invited."

Pisano's assistant snorted. "I know you're a US Navy SEAL. Why are you *really* here?"

Ronin smiled. "I've already answered that question. Why are you so defensive?"

"I care about the Pisanos. I wouldn't want anything to happen to them."

"So, you think you're protecting them by attacking one of their guests?" Ronin raised his eyebrows.

The other man's eyes narrowed. "Call it what you will. I would do anything to protect Marcus Pisano."

What about his daughter? Ronin wanted to ask but didn't.

A softly cleared throat broke the silence between the two men in the room.

Ronin and Costa turned at the same time to find Andre, the butler, standing at the study door. "Mr. and Miss Pisano request Mr. Magnus's presence at the dinner table." He faced Costa. "Should I have another setting placed?"

"No, thank you, Andre. I'm going out." Costa performed a perfect about-face and marched out of the study and across the huge foyer to the front entrance.

Ronin followed Andre back to the dining room, wondering what bug was up Costa's ass that he felt compelled to grill Isabella's fiancé.

CHAPTER 7

As soon as Ronin left the dining room, Isabella turned and paced the length of the dining room, putting distance between her and her father. If he was going to blow a gasket, she didn't want to be within striking distance of his powerful arm.

Not that he'd ever hit her, but there could always be a first time, and she deserved it.

"Father, before you start, let me tell you why I did what I did."

"I'm listening," he said quietly.

She shot a glance over her shoulder.

Instead of the anger she expected to see in his face, she witnessed a deep, heart-wrenching sadness.

"I had to do it." She crossed to him. "So many women were being abused, raped and killed. I couldn't sit back in my gilded palace and let it continue."

"There are armies to handle these things. What did

you hope one woman could do to alleviate the problem?"

"I didn't know what I could do, but I couldn't stand by a moment longer, doing nothing. Asaf trained me to know how to protect myself and how to kill a man."

Her father scrubbed his hand over his face. "But one woman against many barbaric men? I shudder to think what might have happened." He reached out and pulled her into his arms. "I've already lost your mother to cancer. I can't bear to think what those men might have done to you before they killed you and used you as an example to other women who dared to defy them."

Isabella buried her face against her father's strong chest. "That's just it. Some women paid the price for me. I got over one hundred women out of Syria and into refugee camps in Turkey, but there were so many more, who helped me in Syria but are still captives to the ISIS terrorists. And they're being punished for what I did to help them."

"*Mia preziosa bambina*," he said stroking the back of her hair. "You can't fix the world."

"I know that now. But there are one hundred women whose lives will not be governed by ISIS. Women who now have the freedom of choice to live as they see fit." Isabella lifted her head. "I only wish Asaf had made it out of Syria with me. He died to save my life."

Her father nodded. "He was a good soldier and a good man. I would have had words with him about going along with your insane idea. The letters and occasional videos from Africa? How?"

She wrinkled her nose. "I pre-recorded and wrote enough letters to have sent to you for the duration of my stay in Syria. I didn't want you to worry about me."

"I worried. Several times, I scheduled visits to come to you in Africa, but each time, I received word there were contagious sicknesses, or that you had moved deeper into the jungle to teach more children. Your friend always came up with excuses to keep me from coming. And I always received a letter a few days later telling me that you were fine and well." He shook his head. "I had no idea you were in even more hostile territory than Africa." He gripped her arms tightly. "Don't ever do that again. Promise."

She smiled up at her father. "I promise. But I have to do something to help others. We have so much, and there are people all over the world who have lost everything to war, terrorism and natural disasters. I have to help."

"I understand." Her father tucked a strand of her hair behind her ear. "You are so much like your mother. She was always helping others."

Tears stung Isabella's eyes. "She was a good person with a big heart,"

Her father smiled sadly. "A much better person than I can ever hope to be."

"You're not so bad."

"No?" He leaned back. "Tell me about the Navy SEAL you brought home. What's the real story about him?"

Isabella stiffened. She'd already lied to her father about Africa and Syria. She couldn't tell him she'd lied about Ronin. He'd never believe her again. "Ronin is a good man. We're in...love. He's my fiancé." She was stammering and didn't sound very convincing, but lying didn't come easily when it came to her father.

Her father's eyes narrowed. "You love him, you say?"

She looked directly into his eyes. "I do." It was then that she realized how much truth was behind her words. Holy Jesus. She loved Ronin. But how? She'd known him for only a handful of days and most of those had been two years ago. No. It was a mistake. She couldn't have fallen in love that quickly.

"Did you mother ever tell you how we met?"

Thankful her father was taking the spotlight off her and Ronin, she shook her head. "No. Please. Tell me."

"We met at Carnival."

Isabella's eyes widened. Like her and Ronin...

"She was dressed as a beautiful gypsy. I wore a high-wayman's costume, complete with a black mask and a real sword. We danced, we drank and we fell in love that night."

Again, like her and Ronin. "How did you know it was love?"

"I couldn't see myself with anyone else. She was the one person in all of Venice, in all of the world, I could picture at my side for the rest of my life."

"And she felt the same way. I saw it in her eyes every time she looked at you. Mother loved you deeply. She told me she hated dying, because it meant leaving you alone."

"She always thought of others. Never herself."

Isabella sniffed. "Then you understand how I can

love Ronin. We met two years ago at our annual Carnival ball. Here, in this house."

Her father's lips pressed into a thin line. "I'm not certain I trust the boy."

"He's a US Navy SEAL. He lives by a strict code of ethics. He's honorable and true to his word."

"He's also a trained killer."

She smiled gently at her father. "And so is your daughter. I've killed my share of ISIS soldiers. I have blood on my hands."

Her father lifted her hand and pressed a kiss to the back of her knuckles. "Of course, you would be a fierce warrior. I'm sure those who expired at your hands deserved to die."

Isabella's teeth ground together. Images of the atrocities those men had committed flitted through her mind. "They met their just fates and aren't going to heaven to meet a bunch of virgins." She shook herself to free her mind of the darkness still lurking from her time in Syria. "For now, please, accept that Ronin is in my life. He makes me happy. After what I've lived through, I want to feel hopeful for the future. Be happy for me."

Her father nodded. "For you." He nodded to Andre. "Bring the American back to the dinner table."

Andre left the room and returned a few minutes later with Ronin.

Isabella resumed her seat at the table, swiping at her damp cheeks. She hadn't realized how emotional she could get. For the past year, she'd had to fight the tears to hide her true feelings or be considered weak.

Ronin's gaze bounced from her to her father and back again. "Are you all right?" he asked her.

A knot in her throat kept her from answering with words. She nodded and lifted her fork.

"Shall we continue our meal?" Her father took his seat and waited for Ronin to settle beside him. *"Buon appetito."*

The last thing Isabella felt like doing was eating. All she wanted was to climb into bed and curl up next to Ronin. Too many memories flooded over her—too many hollow eyes and faces of desperate women she hadn't been able to save. As her father had said, she couldn't save the world. But she'd given it her best shot.

As soon as the excruciating meal was over, she excused herself and climbed the stairs to her bedroom. Yeah, she'd ditched Ronin, leaving him with her father. But he was a grown man and capable of handling the situation. At that moment, Isabella needed time alone to sort through her feelings about Syria, about her mother and most of all about Ronin.

She loved him.

That, in itself, created a whole new set of problems.

"WHAT IS it you do for the US Navy?" Isabella's father asked, digging into the tiramisu Amina had placed in front of him.

"I'm in special operations," Ronin hedged.

"A SEAL, then." The older man nodded. "I understand the training is grueling and not many men make it through."

Ronin nodded and stuffed a bite of the dessert into his mouth to avoid adding to the description of his BUD/S training.

"What kind of life does a SEAL live?" Another bite of the delicious concoction landed in Pisano's mouth, and he looked up, capturing Ronin's gaze as he chewed.

He threw the older man a bone. "I'm gone a lot on missions."

"Leaving family behind while you go wherever they send you?"

"Yes, sir."

"Which means you'll leave my daughter at home, alone, without protection."

Ronin's jaw stopped in mid-chew, and he swallowed the dessert before he'd completely masticated. "Yes, sir," he said and burst into a coughing fit.

Pisano rose from his chair and stood beside Ronin, pounding his back to expel the inhaled bite of tiramisu.

When he'd recovered his dignity, Ronin said, "I would never put your daughter in danger."

"Intentionally. Oh, I believe that." Her father sat back in his seat. "It's the unintentional consequences I'm more afraid of." He pushed his plate to the side and leaned his elbows on the table. "Oh, I believe you love my daughter and want to be with her, but I don't believe you know the extent to which some people will go to get to my money."

"I have an idea," Ronin disagreed. "But I'm not one of those people who wants your money. I only want your daughter."

"Some things are more precious than money, gold and jewels."

"Agreed," Ronin leaned forward. "Isabella is more precious than all of your money or mansions, fast cars or yachts. She's strong, independent and...special."

Her father nodded, his gaze less guarded and more introspective. "She has a big heart and a sharp mind." His lips turned upward in a smile. "She gets the heart from her mother."

"And her intelligence from you," Ronin concluded. "Speaking of intelligence, I understand you have been the target of some attempts on your life."

Pisano leaned back and crossed his arms over his chest. "I am a wealthy man."

"We've established that."

"Wealth, for some, breeds envy in others."

"True. But who would want to hurt you or your family?"

Isabella's father spread his hands wide. "It could be anyone from foreign governments to members of my own staff." He shook his head. "I don't know."

"When did the current attempts begin?"

Pisano frowned. "You don't need to concern yourself."

"Look, Mr. Pisano. Any concern of Isabella's is a concern of mine. She obviously loves you, and you're her only family. If something were to happen to you, she'd be devastated." He captured the older man's gaze. "Humor me. Maybe I can help."

The older man sighed. "A couple weeks before *mia figlia*—my daughter—returned from her *adventure*, the tea I was served at an upscale restaurant was poisoned."

Ronin waved his hand toward the man. "Yet you're alive and well."

Pisano nodded. "I only had a small sip before I was interrupted by a phone call from one of my major customers. The poison was sufficient to send me to the hospital, but not enough to kill me. I was sick for days, but not dead, thanks to a phone call and the swift response of the medical staff."

"Did you confront the staff of the restaurant?"

Pisano nodded. "The police investigated, and none of the staff admitted to any wrong-doing. Unfortunately, the teabag and the cup had been cleared away from the table immediately upon my departure to make room for other guests."

Ronin nodded. "No evidence."

"Precisely. Then, the day before Isabella arrived in Venice, I was nearly hit by a vehicle that jumped the curb in Rome. At first, I thought it was a drunk driver. In Rome, everyone drives insanely erratic. But, by the way the driver sped off, I could tell he knew exactly what he was doing. I managed to get a license plate number, but the police informed me the car had been stolen that morning. They found it later that day abandoned in an alley. And, before you ask, it had been wiped clean of fingerprints."

"So, two attempts."

"There have been more, but they were so subtle that at the time, I thought they were accidents. Now, I think otherwise. Like the time a motorboat ran into my transport, nearly capsizing us. Or someone bumping into me as I descended the stairs at the opera house one night. I was too busy trying to catch myself to note the description of my attacker."

"You think your bad experiences will become Isabella's fate." It wasn't a question. Ronin's words were a statement.

Pisano nodded. "I now know she's been through worse in Syria." The older man ran his hand down the length of his face, appearing older by the minute. "Had I known she wasn't in Africa, teaching small children to read, I'd have gone after her. As strange as it sounds, I thought she was safe in the jungles of Uganda." He shook his head. "I've raised a very headstrong daughter."

"And done an excellent job. She can hold her own in a fight."

He shook his head. "I suppose I was too buried in my businesses to see what was happening. All I knew was that I missed her terribly."

"I can understand that. I met her two years ago, here in this house, and from that day on, I couldn't get her out of my mind."

Pisano smiled. "She is beautiful like Viviana, her mama."

"Yes, she is." Ronin pushed back from the table. "Sir, while I'm here, I'll do my best to keep your daughter safe."

"And when you're gone?"

Ronin's jaw tightened. "I haven't figured that out yet."

"Based on where she's been for the past year, Isabella

would tell you she can protect herself." Her father shook his head. "But one person cannot be looking all four directions at once."

"True." Ronin had thought the same thing. He had a team of SEALs who had his six. If Isabella gave up her father's protection, she'd be on her own with no one to watch her back.

That was unacceptable.

"I don't know what will happen between your daughter and me, but I care about her. I want you to know that. I would never do anything to harm her."

Isabella's father held his gaze for a long moment. Finally, he nodded. "I believe you. The question is, do you love her enough to walk away?"

"I can't. And I won't," he said, his voice firm.

"Without my men to protect her, she is at high risk of being captured or killed."

"Pardon me, sir, but *your* man took her into Syria where she was at even higher risk of being captured and killed."

Her father gave a twisted smile. "Touché." Then he raised his finger, pointing it at Ronin and pinned him with a wicked glare. "But if you hurt my daughter or break her heart, don't think your SEAL team will keep you safe."

Ronin held up his hand. "I wouldn't worry about me breaking her heart. If anything, she might break mine." On that last note, Ronin rose and walked out of the dining room.

Behind him, he could hear Mr. Pisano's chuckle turn to laughter.

Funny. Ronin didn't find anything to laugh about. Isabella's father was in danger, as well as Isabella on multiple fronts. And Ronin was in danger of a broken heart. All around, the situation sucked. But he didn't want to be in any other place than where he was at that moment.

He hoped he could make a difference in what was going on, maybe even find out who was targeting the Pisano family and neutralize the threat.

CHAPTER 8

WHEN ISABELLA LEFT the dining room, she headed for her bedroom. As she reached the stairs, she changed directions and moved toward the back of the house. She'd take a walk in the garden. She wanted to get outside. The one thing she missed most about Syria was the wide-open heavens, the brightly gleaming stars and complete silence. She'd even found peace in digging her toes in the gritty desert sands.

She knew she wouldn't find the same peace in Venice. The stars would be impossible to see with the glare of street lights washing the sky in color. Nor would she be greeted with the sound of silence. Not during Carnival, with the endless numbers of musicians singing or playing a multitude of instruments. Not to mention the delighted squeals and laughter of people enjoying the sights and sounds of the most raucous time of the year. But the garden behind the mansion was full of the roses her mother had insisted on planting and the fountains she'd taken great pleasure in choosing and having installed.

At that moment, Isabella was missing her mother as much as the day she'd passed away. The garden was the one place she felt closest to her.

Once outside, she inhaled deeply. The heavy aroma of roses filled her senses, making her feel as if her mother were there, wrapping her arms around her entire body. Instead of starlight, she was surrounded by twinkle lights her father had installed to light the garden path, creating a fairyland of hopes and wishes. Or so her mother had described it.

It was a magical place that never ceased to lift her spirits. Even the strident laughter and shouts on the other side of the wall couldn't dim the beauty of her mother's garden.

Isabella sat on the bench beneath the climbing rose arbor at the end of the path and closed her eyes. The only thing that could make the moment better was if Ronin would join her and wrap real, muscular arms around her.

She looked over her shoulder and sighed with disappointment. He hadn't followed her. Her father had likely kept him at the table, grilling him for answers to his entire life story.

Her lips twitched.

Poor Ronin.

He hadn't known what he was getting into by coming back to Venice. Now, he was cornered in a mansion that could be more like a prison, surrounded by people who wanted to boss him around and ask too many questions.

She shrugged and lifted her face to the heavens, inhaling deeply. *Mother, if you're there, please help me figure out this mess.*

And by mess, she needed to know how to void the price on her head, placed there by an incensed ISIS leader. The only way for that to go away would be for the ISIS leader to die a sudden death. Then, perhaps, his followers would forget she existed and leave her alone.

But then there was the matter of the attacks on the Pisano family. She needed to ask her father what that was all about. Was he in danger? Did she need to do her own investigation to find the culprit? Had the police done anything?

Questions spun through her head until she couldn't sit still another moment. She leaped to her feet and turned toward the house, only to walk into a wall of stone.

She bounced off and would have fallen backward over the bench if hands hadn't reached out to grip her arms.

"Are you all right?" Ronin asked.

"Yes. Of course." Heat rose in Isabella's cheeks, and her knees shook at his nearness. The man had a lethal effect on her ability to focus. "I didn't see you."

Ronin chuckled. "Obviously." He didn't let go of her arms. Instead, he gathered her closer and wrapped her in his embrace.

She rested her cheek against his chest, listening to

the reassuring thump of his heartbeat. "Did my father run you through the inquisition?"

His chuckle rumbled beneath her ear. "Some."

"And you didn't run screaming from the house?" She tipped back her head and stared up into his eyes.

Ronin shook his head. "Everything I want is here. Why would I run from it? From you."

Her eyes narrowed. "You really shouldn't do that."

"Do what?"

"Make me sad."

"How have I made you sad?"

"When you say things like that, you make me wish for more than I can have."

"Like what?" He pulled her closer, crushing her hips against his. The evidence of his desire nudged her belly.

She traced the buttons on his shirt up his chest and stopped when she touched his lips. "Like you."

"Babe, you don't even have to ask. I'm all yours." He sucked her finger between his teeth and bit down gently.

Isabella jerked back her hand. "Hey, that finger is attached." Her heart swelled inside her chest. His words made her long for a simpler world, one where she could leave with him and not worry about ISIS or kidnapping threats. But that wasn't her life. "You know we have to break up soon, don't you?"

He bent to nibble her earlobe. "While you were confessing your role in Syria to your father, why didn't you tell him the truth about us?"

"I couldn't admit to lying to him two times in a row. He'd never trust me again. Besides, he already knew about Syria. I'm surprised he waited to say anything until now."

"A lie is a lie when you're talking to someone you profess to love."

Isabella's shoulders sagged. "You're right. But I'm all the family he has. If he can't trust me, who *can* he trust?" She looked up at him, her eyes widening, her body tensing. "You didn't tell him the truth, did you?"

He shrugged, his lips twisting into a teasing smile. "I couldn't. If I told him, you'd have no need to keep me around. Your father would have me thrown out on the street faster than you can say *mia familia.*"

Isabella relaxed, glad he hadn't told her secret. And happier still he hadn't been thrown out of the house. She could have him for the full two weeks of his leave, if she chose to. They didn't have to stage their breakup until the end of that time.

She wrapped her arms around his waist and pressed her cheek to his chest, inhaling the distinct scent of Ronin Magnus. His was a cross between the musk of his own skin and the spicy cologne he wore.

Isabella loved it. She'd kept one of the T-shirts he'd left in the hotel two years ago and slept with it until she'd left for Africa. His scent lingered for months. She'd left it in one of her bottom drawers in her closet for her return. But now, she had something even better.

Ronin.

She hugged him tightly.

He kissed the top of her head and chuckled. "What happened to staging the breakup?"

"We have time. No need to hurry it up." She tipped

her head up. "You're not leaving for another week and a few days, right?"

"Right."

"We can plan on breaking up then."

His lips twitched. "In the meantime, we're a happily engaged couple." He bent and scooped her into his arms. "I don't know about you, but all this fresh air is making me sleepy. Shouldn't we go to bed?"

She laughed. "As long as sleep isn't what you have in mind."

He carried her all the way through the garden, into the house, where they ran into her father in the massive foyer at the base of the stairs.

"Father," Isabella bleated, immediately embarrassed.

His eyebrows rose sharply. "Isabella!"

RONIN LOWERED Isabella's legs to the ground. "Pardon us, sir. We were just..."

Isabella smoothed her dress and straightened her shoulders. "We were just turning in for the night. Is there anything I can get you before we go upstairs?"

Her father glared at Ronin, but then his face softened as he turned his attention to Isabella. "You can give your father a kiss."

Isabella grinned and leaned upward on her toes to kiss the old man's cheek. "*Ti amo, Papa.*"

"*Ti amo, mia bambina.*" He engulfed her in a bear hug and kissed the top of her hair. "Sleep well." His glance narrowed on Ronin. "And I mean sleep."

"Yes, Father," she said, her gaze lowering.

"Remember, we have the parade tomorrow and the ball tomorrow night."

Isabella frowned. "You shouldn't be involved in the parade or the ball. Not with all that's going on."

"What do you know about what's going on?" Pisano glared over her head at Ronin.

Ronin shrugged. "I haven't said anything."

"No, he hasn't," Isabella said. "But 'little birds' told me about the incidents. You shouldn't go out in that crowd. You don't know what might happen."

"I refuse to be held captive in my own home. If someone wants at me, let them."

Isabella snorted. "Now, you know how I feel."

Her father straightened to his full height, which was level with Ronin's. "I have Lorenzo, Matteo—and Andre, if we need him. They will keep me safe."

She shook her head. "If you go out, I'm going out."

"And count me in," Ronin added. "Hopefully, there will be safety in numbers."

"I don't like the idea of you going out in the Carnival crowd." Her father stared down at her, perhaps trying to intimidate her with his heavy frown.

"And I don't like the idea of you going out there." Isabella crossed her arms over her chest and frowned back at her father.

Ronin fought the urge to laugh at them, knowing it would not be received well. The two Pisanos were as stubborn as they came.

Finally, her father nodded. "Very well. You'll both need costumes. I'll have Andre provide something appropriate."

"No horse heads or dog masks."

"I won't wear a mask," Ronin insisted.

"It's part of the Carnival experience," Mr. Pisano said.

"Not part of mine. If anything, I'll wear a cloth mask like a bandit or Zorro," Ronin offered. I don't want anything to impair my vision."

Pisano nodded. "I'll inform Andre."

"*Buona notte, Papa.*" Isabella gave her father another kiss on the cheek and started up the stairs.

Ronin took a step after her but was stopped by the older Pisano's hand on his arm. "You will treat my daughter with respect."

"Yes, sir," Ronin replied. A chuckle from above made him want to smile, but he held it in until Isabella's father released his arm and walked away.

Ronin took the steps two at a time to catch up with Isabella.

"Does my father frighten you?" she asked, giving him a sideways glance.

"Not in the least. He's only doing what any father would do for a daughter as beautiful as you." Ronin kissed the tip of her nose and once again swung her up into his arms. "Now, where were we?"

He ran up the remainder of the steps without breaking a sweat or breathing hard. Isabella was light for being as tall as she was.

When they entered her room, she wrapped her arms around his neck and kissed him on the lips. "That's for not making me feel less capable or in the least diminished by carrying me up the stairs."

He suppressed a smile. "I wouldn't do that."

"I know. That's why I l-like you so much. I like that you make me feel feminine without taking away my independence or lording it over me with your strength."

"After your time in Syria, I can imagine you could take me down and slit my throat before I could cry uncle." He winked. "Don't feel obligated to demonstrate. I'm a believer."

She laughed and flung her arms around him. Then she pushed him backward onto the bed.

He loved it when she took the lead and loved it even more when he made her come.

They made love throughout the night and into the early hours of the morning.

When Ronin finally fell asleep, he rested deeply, at home with Isabella curled up against his body.

It seemed as though he'd just closed his eyes when the pounding began. He opened them and stared up at the ornate chandelier hanging from the ceiling. "What the hell?" he said into the gray light of early morning. He sat up and stared at lilac walls, filmy-white curtains and gilt-framed paintings adorning the bedroom. A window overlooked the canal below, busy with the morning traffic of small motor boats, carrying goods and people into and out of the water-bound city.

Isabella was already up and pulling on her clothes. "*Buongiorno.*" She smiled broadly.

He stifled a groan and lay back down. "Is it morning already?"

"We have a lot to do today. Starting with a quick breakfast and then dressing for the parade. Get up."

"Nag." Ronin rolled away from her. "You should have thought of that before you kept me up all night."

She threw a pillow at him. "You can sleep tomorrow. Today is a big day for the Carnival and the Pisano house. My father is a prominent figure in the riverboat parade. We have to hurry to get there."

Ronin rolled out of the bed and stretched, standing naked with the sunlight just edging through the open window.

Isabella stopped in her efforts to dress and stared. "Are you just trying to delay our appearance at the breakfast table?" She licked her lips.

He winked and stretched again, flexing the muscles across his chest and abdomen. "Is it working?"

She threw another pillow at him. "Yes. Now, be serious. We have a lot to do today."

He grabbed her around the middle and pulled her against his hard body and even harder erection. "Can we fit in one more thing?"

She stilled, her face flushing pink. "Well…"

He smacked her bottom and twirled her away. "Too late. We have to get to breakfast before your father comes looking for us and finds us still in bed, making mad, passionate love."

"Oooo," she growled. "You're irritating."

"Like an itch you can't scratch?"

"Exactly." She retrieved a pillow from the floor and hit him in the gut with one end. "Next time you tease me, be prepared to follow through."

"Bella, I'm always prepared to follow through with you." He waggled his eyebrows and laughed. He might not have gotten much sleep, but the fact he'd get to spend the day with Isabella made up for that.

His happy mood persisted until he got a load of the costume Andre had left outside the bedroom door.

CHAPTER 9

ISABELLA COULD BARELY BREATHE. The corset fit so tightly around her middle her lungs worked at only half their capacity. All in the name of Carnival, the annual festival held in Venice. Thousands of tourists would be crowding the waterways and streets, dressed in elaborate costumes, singing and dancing.

All she had to do was make it through the parade of boats and the march through Piazza San Marco. Her father would make a short speech, and then they could all go back home, get out of their costumes and relax for a few hours before the ball.

If she survived the heavy layers of russet fabric in the one of the most elaborate Renaissance dresses she'd ever worn. Her headpiece alone must have weighed fifteen pounds with yards of ribbon trimmed in gold glitter. She had chosen not to wear the full porcelain face mask, opting for one that covered only the top half of her face.

The gown was stunning, the mask was even more elaborate, but she would rather be wearing her blue jeans and a comfortable T-shirt. Even a roomy burka would be preferable to the corset and heavy clothing.

She sat in the boat beside her father as they floated slowly along the Grand Canal in a procession of hundreds of boats, their destination the square at San Marco where the opening ceremonies would herald the official beginning of Carnival and its week of festivities.

Her father sat beside her wearing a long purple velvet coat. Beneath it, he wore a white shirt with full sleeves and lace at the cuffs. On his head was a long wig of white curls and a tri-corner hat. He looked so handsome and distinguished, like the American George Washington on his way to a fancy gathering.

Isabella glanced behind her at Ronin, wearing a black cape, black tights and a long red tunic. His face was partially covered by a strip of black fabric Andre had fashioned into a mask.

Isabella's heart fluttered. He was just as handsome in this more elaborate costume, as he had been in his hastily thrown-together costume of two years ago. The clothes weren't what made him so attractive. It was the way he held himself, straight and proud.

If only she were just another tourist, perhaps a French woman there only for the festivities before she returned to her home in rural France, where no one would chase after her to claim the price on her head. If only she could lead a simple life, work as a baker or an accountant.

What would it be like to be married to a US Navy

SEAL and live in the U.S.? That fantasy seemed so far from Italy and her life here. They could live in an apartment or maybe a cottage in Virginia. That's where Ronin had said his unit was based.

She could get a job as a waitress or volunteer at soup kitchen. Wasn't that what Navy wives did? Or she could go to college in the U.S. and get a certificate to teach children.

She sat up straighter. Would the school directors allow the Angel of Mercy, who'd fought against ISIS, to teach small children to read and write? Would they learn of her involvement in Syria and ban her from being anywhere near a school?

Isabella sighed, her gaze constantly sweeping over the occupants of the other crafts and the people lined up on the docks and landings along the Grand Canal, witnessing the procession.

Were there ISIS operatives hiding among the Carnival-goers, waiting for their moment to strike her down, or capture her to return her to al-Jahashi? Wearing this dress, she couldn't begin to outrun anyone, and she doubted she had the flexibility to effectively defend herself. She'd be an easy target, waiting for someone to take her out. Her only saving grace was the width of the cloak and the skirt. Sure, they could hit the costume, it was large enough. The shooter would have to be completely incompetent to miss. But whether the bullets would hit her person was another question.

Lorenzo sat on the other side of her father and two bodyguards, whose names she couldn't recall, sat in the front of the boat.

Andre steered the craft while Ronin and Matteo sat on the rear bench, covering Isabella and her father's backs.

The water parade went off without a hitch. One by one, the passengers in the boats pulled up to the dock, the passengers disembarked and the boat drivers poled the boats away to tie them up alongside the rows of buildings. Andre pulled their boat up to the landing and waited as Lorenzo and Ronin assisted Isabella and her father from the craft.

Once steady on her feet, Isabella hooked her father's arm and led the way into Piazza San Marco. A huge crowd had gathered. With the upcoming costume contest looming, people filled the square wearing some of the most flamboyant costumes in every color under the rainbow. Most wore fine, white porcelain masks and elaborate headdresses.

The music was as loud and boisterous as the people playing and dancing to it.

Carnival was Isabella's favorite time of the Venetian year. The outfits were outlandish and many times garish. But she didn't care. The people were there to have fun.

Getting through the crowd proved to be more difficult than she remembered. With the wide spread of her gown, she couldn't get close enough to people to jostle them out of the way.

Her father, in his much narrower costume had no difficulties at all elbowing his way through the crowd. He had Lorenzo at his side, guarding him from unanticipated attacks.

"Go on," she urged. "You have to get to the dais to make your speech. I'll only slow you down." She released her father's elbow and nodded toward the stage. "Go and dazzle them with your brilliance. I'll catch up."

"I won't leave you," her father said.

"I have Ronin." She held out her hand.

Ronin took it and slipped his other hand around her waist, beneath the cape. "I'll keep her close," he promised.

Her father frowned, glanced toward the dais and nodded. "I will only be a moment." With Lorenzo's help, he nudged and edged his way through the crowd, finally making it to the platform with the podium.

With Lorenzo close at his side, he climbed up the stairs to the dais and waited to be announced.

Isabella panned the crowd, searching for anyone with a gun, praying her father would get through his speech quickly and get down off that stage. When he stepped out in front of the crowd, he would be at his most vulnerable.

The master of ceremonies waved him forward. Isabella held her breath and listened for any sound even vaguely similar to the pop of gunfire. The crowd cheered, and then quieted while her father spoke.

He made his statement clear, short and to the point. When he finished, the crowd cheered, the music played and her father left the stage on his own two feet. He hadn't been shot. He hadn't even been heckled.

A smile slipped across Isabella's face. So far, so good.

They just had the trip back to her father's mansion to navigate, and they could get out of the costumes and breathe.

As her father and Lorenzo slowly made their way back toward Isabella and Ronin, the music grew louder and the people twisted and turned, dancing and laughing.

For a moment, Isabella lost sight of her father. "Do you see him?"

"No," Ronin responded. He rose on his toes. "I can't see anything past the headdresses and hats."

For a brief moment, she caught sight of Lorenzo in his white, Elizabethan gentleman's tunic and tights, and then nothing again.

Her pulse sped, and her hands grew damp as she twisted them in front of her. Isabella was near the point she was ready to strip out of the dress and dive into the crowd to find her father when he emerged and she caught sight of him.

He was smiling and laughing at something Lorenzo said.

A jester in a bright green and purple costume danced by her father swinging his arms like a propeller. His costume and the colors were so engaging, Isabella found herself watching him as he passed her father, instead of keeping an eye on the older Pisano.

When she looked back at her father, he was leaning heavily on Lorenzo, one of his hands clutching at his belly where a bright red stain spread across the crisp white shirt beneath his purple coat.

Isabella cried out and ran toward him, tripping over her massive skirts.

Ronin slipped a hand around her waist and steadied her, running at her side.

When they reached Lorenzo and her father, her father had pulled the mask from his face and slumped against his bodyguard, his own face as white as the mask he'd removed.

"Lay him on the ground," Isabella commanded. She shot a glance at Ronin. "Find that jester."

Ronin shook his head. "I won't leave you."

"Find him," she bit out.

Andre appeared beside Ronin. "Go. I think he headed toward the north entrance to the square."

Ronin hesitated a moment longer.

"Please," Isabella begged. "He cannot be allowed to do this again."

Ronin left Isabella and ran into the crowd.

"Apply pressure to the wound," she ordered Lorenzo. He hesitated.

"Do it, or he'll bleed to death!"

Lorenzo pressed the palm of his hand into the bloody gash.

Her father winced and passed out.

Good. At least while he was out, he wouldn't be in as much pain.

Isabella lifted her skirt and ripped fabric from her white petticoat, making long strips. She folded one of the strips into a neat square and nudged Lorenzo aside.

The man lifted his bloody hand away from the wound and more blood spilled out onto the ground.

Isabella ripped open her father's shirt, quickly assessed the injury and pressed the pad of fabric over the slice in his belly. Holding the pressure steady, she glanced around at the onlookers.

A policeman pushed his way through the crowd and dropped to his knees beside her. "An ambulance is on the way."

"Thank God," she whispered. She fought back the ready tears pooling in her eyes. This man was her only relative. If he died, she'd have no one else in the world.

Her thoughts went to Ronin. He wanted her but, given the situation, she couldn't wish her life on him. She prayed she hadn't sent him into the jaws of danger.

As the minutes dragged on waiting for the paramedics and the water ambulance to arrive at the landing, all Isabella had were her thoughts to keep her company. Her father remained unconscious, and Lorenzo seemed to be in shock over the amount of blood.

Isabella's time in Syria had hardened her to the sight of blood, but when it was someone you loved, it was still pretty horrific.

Please let Ronin return alive. Please.

RONIN RIPPED the mask from his face and ran, pushing and shoving his way through the crowd. Twice he thought he'd found the jester, and twice he'd been wrong. The colors in the costume weren't right. They needed to be purple and green, not orange and red or yellow and blue.

He was about to give up and return to Isabella and her father when he spotted a man wearing the green and purple pantaloons he'd seen on the jester who'd attacked Marcus Pisano. The man had shed the jacket and wore a white shirt. He'd ditched the headdress he'd been wearing somewhere along the way, leaving his head bare but for a dark swath of hair.

He glanced over his shoulder again and again, while running toward the north entrance.

With the majority of the revelers occupied at the center of the square, the crowd thinned on the northern edge.

Ronin raced after the attacker, dodging women in voluminous dresses and men in big hats.

The jester ducked down an alley, disappearing into the shadows.

Determined to capture the man who'd stabbed Isabella's father, Ronin burst free of the throng and ran full out, charging into the alley, wishing he held his M4A1 rifle. The only weapons he had were his hands, but he'd do whatever it took to stop the man from harming Isabella and her family. With drums pounding, cymbals clanging and music blasting through loudspeakers behind him, Ronin blocked out the noise and focused on his target.

Coming from the bright Italian sunshine to the darkness of the alley didn't give Ronin's vision time to adjust. He couldn't see anything but the archway at the end.

He didn't want to lose his target in the twists and turns of the maze-like alleyways and canals. Ronin shot ahead, racing through a tunnel of darkness to the opening at the end and nearly plunged over the edge of a drop-off into a canal. He stopped short, teetering on the lip of a landing his hands going up to catch the arched bricks overhead. When he had his balance, he dropped his arms and took stock of where he was.

The tunnel ended at the canal. The only way out was by boat or swimming.

He caught a glimpse of the tail of a motor boat rounding the next corner in the canal. The man he'd been chasing hadn't had time to start a boat, much less get to the next corner in the short moments before Ronin arrived. But he could have had someone there waiting for him.

If only Ronin had a boat to follow.

Leaning out, he peered over the edge in case there was a ledge beneath where he was standing. No boat, but at that exact moment, a body floated to the surface of the murky canal water.

Ronin jumped back, his heart leaping into his throat. Holy hell, the man he'd been chasing lay face down in the water, his green and purple pants barely visible beneath the surface.

"What the hell?" Ronin shrugged out of the frilly costume jacket, dropped into the water and dragged the man to the lower landing where boats could tie off. All he saw on the fellow's back was a small hole in his shirt.

Ronin flipped him over to find a gaping bullet hole in his chest. He'd been shot, and the bullet had made a mess of his insides. More than likely he'd died before he hit the water.

The only good thing about the scenario was that he wouldn't be stabbing another member of the Pisano family.

The bad thing was someone had shot him, and it appeared they'd done it to shut him up.

CHAPTER 10

Isabella rode with her father to the emergency room at the nearest trauma center and waited while he was examined and the doctor sutured the wound closed. By the time they were finished, it was past noon and Ronin still had not surfaced.

Isabella worried. Had he found the attacker? Had the attacker struck him with the same knife with which he'd cut her father?

She focused on calming her rampant thoughts with less bloody scenarios. Ronin probably didn't know where they were or how to speak enough Italian to get directions. Although he'd been practicing his Italian over the past two years, it didn't mean he could understand all its nuances.

Isabella held her father's hand in hers, studying the dried blood on his fingers, thankful the knife hadn't hit any vital organs.

The man had lost blood, but not enough to keep him from giving his report to the detective who came to question him about the man who'd stabbed him. Once the detective left, her father could not be held down.

He blustered at the doctor and nurses, complaining that they were taking too much time, and didn't they know what night it was? "I have to get back to my home. There are preparations to finalize for the masquerade ball at the Pisano mansion. My guests expect me to be there to welcome them."

"You're not welcoming anyone tonight," the doctor said. "You need to cancel the event."

"Agreed," Isabella said. "Even the doctor knows you're not up to a party."

"I can't break tradition or disappoint the guests. Besides, the party doesn't need me to be there for the guests to enjoy the festivities. I can stay in my rooms, as long as someone acts as host to all those people." He puffed out his chest. "It's a Pisano tradition your mother started all those years ago. She would never have cancelled." He looked up at Isabella. "I've never missed one since Viviana insisted on the first, over twenty-five years ago." He squeezed Isabella's hand. "If she hadn't died, she would have been there."

To keep her father from becoming agitated and morose, Isabella nodded. "Fine, Papa. I'll be there to carry on the Pisano tradition. But you are going home to bed."

"Pisanos do not wallow in bed," he groused.

"They do if they want to give their bodies time to heal and get well." When he opened his mouth to protest, she held up her hand. "I'll greet the guests, *if* you promise to stay in your rooms."

His lips pressed together in a tight line, and he frowned mightily. Then he sighed and nodded. "All right. But only if you promise to stay with your fiancé or one of the bodyguards throughout the night. I don't know what I'd do if I lost my only daughter."

"I'm not going anywhere, Papa." She patted his hand and stood. Her gaze drifted to the door. Still no sign of Ronin.

"He's a US Navy SEAL," her father said, as if reading her mind. "He'll be fine."

"I know, Papa, but I can't help worrying."

"You really love him, don't you?" he asked.

She turned to face her father and nodded. "I do. But there are so many reasons why we shouldn't be together."

"And only one reason why you should." Her father's eyes misted. "The same reason your mother and I married...love."

Isabella closed her eyes as tears stung the backs of her lids. "But is it enough? ISIS wants me dead. Your enemies will continue to target you and me as long as—"

"As long as I have money for ransom." He nodded. "I could give away all my money and solve that problem."

She shook her head. "You worked too hard to build your empire. Besides, Pisanos don't give up."

"Family is more important," her father said. "Your mother taught me that."

"And she also taught you that money can't buy

everything." Her breath caught in her throat. No matter how many doctors her father had taken her mother to, none of them could take away the cancer. None of them could keep her alive. She'd died despite all the specialists her father brought in on her case, despite all the drugs they'd employed.

"Money isn't everything," her father whispered, looking down at his hands, the lines in his face deeper, the shadows in his eyes darker than Isabella had ever remembered seeing.

Isabella laid her hand on his. "You still miss her, don't you?"

"Every day of my life."

Every day she'd been in Syria, she'd thought of Ronin, wondering where he was in the world. He could have been in the same country, and she'd never have known. All the while she'd told herself, she'd done the right thing by letting him go, but her heart had told her a different story. He was the one for her. They felt right together.

"Oh, thank God," a deep voice said behind her. "Isabella, I finally found you."

She turned and fell into Ronin's arms. "I thought you'd never get here."

"I had to talk to police and detectives. I couldn't get away sooner." He pulled her into his arms and held her close. "How's your father?"

"I'll live," her father said. "If someone will get me out of here."

Isabella laughed. "He's irritable and wants to go home. We're waiting on his release instructions."

Ronin led Isabella over to the bed and stared down at her father. "Vital organs?"

"Safe," her father said.

"Good." Ronin nodded. "Bleeding stopped?"

Her father gingerly touched the bandage on his belly. "Yes."

"Good," Ronin repeated.

"The attacker?" Isabella asked.

"Dead."

"I TURNED the body over to the police and had to go to the station to answer questions. Otherwise, I would have been here sooner." Ronin had been fit to be tied by the time he'd left the station. "Thankfully, the police located the hospital they brought your father to. I got here quickly but had a hard time communicating with the people at the front desk." He grimaced. "My Italian's a little more rusty than I thought."

"But you found us, you're all right and that's what matters." Isabella hugged him around the middle. She still wore the flamboyant costume, sans the elaborate headdress. Her own hair hung around her shoulders in long dark waves. God, she was beautiful.

"What matters is your father is going to live." He kissed the top of her head and nodded to Mr. Pisano. "It could have been a lot worse."

"Did they identify the assailant?" Pisano asked.

Ronin nodded. "He was a Syrian refugee they'd been watching. They suspect he had ties to ISIS."

Isabella froze in the curve of his arm.

Her father shook his head. "You can't blame yourself, Isabella."

"How can I not?" She took a step away from Ronin. "Don't you see? Stabbing you could have been a warning to me."

"Or he could have been paid by someone else to do the deed," Ronin offered. "I didn't kill the man. He was already dead when I found him face down in the canal. Someone put a bullet through him. A boat was getting away when I caught up with the guy."

Both the older Pisano and Isabella frowned heavily.

"Someone shot him," Isabella said, more as a statement than a question.

"At pointblank range, based on the hole in his chest," Ronin supplied.

Mr. Pisano's gaze met Ronin's. "Whoever hired him obviously didn't want the man to talk."

The door to the room burst open and Niccolo rushed in, speaking in Italian.

From what Ronin could make out, he was thankful to locate the man and that he was alive.

"Speak in English, please," Pisano said.

Niccolo shot an irritated glance at Ronin and continued in English. "I was at the office when I heard and came immediately." He stared at his boss, his gaze running the man's length. "What did the doctors say?"

Pisano nodded. "I will live."

Niccolo released a huge sigh. "Thankfully. What happened?"

"It appears someone might have been paid to stab

my father and run." Isabella reached for her father's hand. "The question is why?"

"No, the more important question is why I have not been released from this hospital." Her father sat up in the bed and winced. "Hand me my clothes."

Isabella complied.

The man didn't wait for anyone to clear the room. Instead, he swung his bare legs over the side of the hospital bed and jammed them into the fancy pants he'd worn at the parade. "I'd give half my fortune for a proper pair of trousers," he grumbled.

"You'll have to make do until we get home." Isabella helped him into the shirt, leaving the front open. Then she bent to assist him into his shoes.

By that time, the nurse returned with his release instructions advising him to rest and take antibiotics to keep infection from setting in.

The trip back to his Venetian mansion was slow and arduous as they worked their way through the canals crowded with revelers.

When they reached the Pisano estate, Ronin and Andre half-carried, half-walked Mr. Pisano up the stairs to his second-floor suite. Isabella and Andre took over from there, getting her father dressed in comfortable clothes, tending his wound and settling him into his bed.

From outside the bedchamber, Ronin could hear the older Pisano grumbling and grousing throughout the process.

Andre descended the stairs and returned with a tray

of tea and biscuits to wash down the painkillers and sleeping aid.

In the meantime, Ronin took the opportunity to shower the canal water off his body and out of his hair and put on a clean pair of jeans, not the tights and costume he'd been wearing when he dove into the canal. He hated leaving Isabella for even a minute. With someone willing to pay someone to stab Mr. Pisano, and then kill him to keep him silent, the stakes had just gotten significantly higher. Couple that with a houseful of workers, decorating the historic mansion for the annual ball, and the possibility of another attack seemed not only possible but probable.

He caught Isabella backing out of her father's suite, talking as she went.

"I will, Papa. Don't worry. Ronin and Lorenzo will be by my side all evening. The ball will continue as always." She closed the door, heaved a huge sigh and turned. She had removed the huge gown and wore only the torn petticoat and chemise. Her dark hair hung past her shoulders in wild disarray, and her cheeks were pink from exertion.

Ronin caught her arms and pulled her against him. "Did I hear right?"

"What did you hear?" She smiled up at him, her lips so tempting, it was all Ronin could do not to kiss them.

"That the ball will go on as planned?"

She nodded, resting her hands on his chest. "I made a deal with my father. If he stayed in his room all evening, I would greet the guests."

Ronin shook his head. "It's too dangerous." He touched a finger to her lips. "And don't say you can take care of yourself."

She moved his finger with one of her own. "I can take care of myself. But I will also have you and Lorenzo to be my eyes and ears in case I miss anything." Isabella stared up into his eyes. "That is presumptuous of me." She smiled. "I haven't even asked if you would accompany me to the ball."

"You know I'll go wherever you go. You don't have to ask." He clutched her body against his and bent to kiss her. "But I don't feel good about this. Though the man who stabbed your father is dead, there's someone out there who still means business." He kissed her forehead, and then pressed his lips to her eyelids and the tip of her nose. Finally, he hovered over her mouth. "I can't lose you."

"You won't," she whispered, her breath warm on his mouth. "We'll have to be vigilant."

He claimed her mouth and would have thrust his tongue past her lips if a noise behind him hadn't alerted him to someone else's presence.

"What are we being vigilant about?" a voice interrupted from the landing.

Ronin stepped back from Isabella to face Pisano's assistant, irritation making his lips press together in a tight line. The man had crappy timing. "Costa."

The man nodded. "Magnus."

"It isn't polite to sneak up on people," Isabella chastised, smoothing back her hair from her face.

"How is your father?" Costa asked.

"He should be asleep by now," she responded. "He is not to be disturbed. Andre will be with him throughout the remainder of the day and evening."

Niccolo nodded. "Business will wait."

She nodded. "Exactly. Nothing is so important it can't wait until the weekend is over and my father has had sufficient time to recover." Isabella moved past him. "Now, if you'll excuse me, I have to check on preparations."

Ronin followed her down the stairs into the massive front foyer where the guests would be met later that evening.

Men and women were busy decorating the walls and banisters with flowers, lights and yards of ribbon. They set out chairs along the sides and were erecting a dais in one corner for the musicians.

Isabella met with the woman in charge and spoke to her in Italian, rattling off instructions too fast for Ronin to keep up.

The woman nodded and went back to work, directing her workers.

Isabella marched through the hallway and dining room, and into a large kitchen bustling with men and women in white coats and chef's hats. She spoke with the man who appeared to be in charge. He nodded and went back to work.

Isabella turned to Ronin. "We have a couple of hours before the festivities begin. I suggest we eat now. We might not get the chance to later."

Ronin's belly rumbled. He hadn't realized time had blown past noon, and they hadn't stopped long enough to have lunch. Though he could go a couple days without a meal, he preferred to power up while he could. Situations changed quickly, and he might need the energy boost for later that evening. Preferably after the guests left. "How long does the party last?"

Isabella gave him a twisted grin. "Until the last person leaves. It usually equates to all night."

Ronin sighed. So much for needing energy for more pleasurable pursuits. At least he'd be with Isabella throughout the ordeal, even if it wasn't in her bed, making sweet love to her.

If the crowd he'd seen that morning at the opening ceremonies was any indication, tonight, the room would be packed. He'd have to stay close or risk leaving her exposed to another sneak attack.

Ronin insisted on eating at the table in the kitchen. They didn't need the staff to take too much time out of their preparations for the evening's events.

The chef prepared a light meal for them consisting of a delicious lentil soup and *paninis* stuffed full of a variety of meats and cheeses. They washed the food down with some of the best red wine Ronin had ever tasted. As someone who preferred beer and whiskey, he found that he could easily become a convert to Italian wine.

When he thought the meal couldn't be tastier, the chef provided a delicate French pastry covered in powdered sugar. The morsel melted in Ronin's mouth.

When he kissed Isabella afterward, he could taste the sugar on her lips, and the flavor was all the sweeter.

She wiped her fingers on her napkin and pushed away from the table. "The musicians will arrive in less than an hour, and the guests will be begin trickling in shortly afterward. I'm sorry, but the dress for the evening will be costumes."

Ronin nodded. "Anything for the hostess."

"At least you don't have to wear one of those ridiculously heavy dresses. I could not have survived during the Renaissance."

He grimaced. "If I had to wear tights all the time, neither could I."

"But you have such sexy legs." She winked and stepped past him, reaching out to pinch his butt.

"Hey." Ronin rubbed the spot and laughed. "Two can play that game."

"Then we'd better hurry or we won't have time." She ran past the workers in the hallway and foyer and up the stairs in her chemise and petticoat, her hair flying behind her, her laughter echoing off the walls and ceilings.

Ronin raced after her, his heart lighter than it had been in years. He pushed the worry to the back of his mind. For that moment, they were a young couple in love, about to make love, and that's all he needed to know. The evening would arrive soon enough. Then he'd slip back into tactical mode. If you could call wearing tights and a sissy costume tactical. He wished he had his SEAL team around him for what promised to be a very long night. Or his brothers who were equally trained in combat skills. Mack, Wyatt and Sam would have had his back and helped him protect Isabella.

But what about when he left? Isabella's father had nailed that question. What happened to Isabella when Ronin deployed? Who would protect her? He wouldn't be there.

CHAPTER 11

FOR THE NEXT HOUR, Isabella basked in the attentions of her SEAL fiancé, pushing aside all the tasks that awaited her for her selfish indulgence in mind-blowing sex.

The near-miss with her father had brought home to her that nothing was forever. You had to grab for happiness while you could.

Lying in Ronin's arms, she was the happiest she'd ever been, and she refused to think of a future without him by her side. She knew it was inevitable, but she wouldn't think about it. Not now. Not when they would spend a magical evening dancing and laughing at the crazy costumes and antics of the guests who came to the annual ball.

Though she'd rather be alone with Ronin, she would be proud to have him standing by her side, greeting guests with her. He was a handsome man. His broad chest and sexy legs would make her the envy of every woman.

Satiated after making love, she brushed a kiss across Ronin's lips, and then rolled out of the bed.

Ronin groaned. "Is it that time?"

"It is," she responded from the bathroom. Isabella reached into the shower and turned on the water, adjusting the temperature. She wrapped her hair in a towel and stepped beneath the spray.

Hands encircled around her from behind and pulled her against a solid, muscular body.

"Mmm." She reached behind her and cupped his buttocks. "If we had a little more time…"

"It doesn't take much," he encouraged.

"No?" Isabella turned in his arms.

He held up a condom. "I came prepared."

"So you did." She took the packet from him, tore it open and rolled the protection over his cock.

Without hesitation, he scooped her up by the backs of her thighs, wrapped her legs around his waist and pressed her back against the cool marble tiles.

"You are amazing," he said and slid into her, burying himself in her channel.

Her muscles tightened around him, squeezing tight, holding him there for a long moment.

Then he backed out and rammed back into her, settling into a steady rhythm that had her panting by the time they finally climaxed together.

Once he had his breathing under control, Ronin pulled free and lowered her legs to the ground. "Amazing." He kissed her, peeled off the condom and disposed of it then returned to lather soap over every inch of her body. By the time he'd made his way halfway down, she was on fire, with steam rising from her damp flesh. When he finished and rinsed her off, her knees wobbled, and she could barely stand.

Her competitive streak insisted on returning the favor.

Isabella explored every one of his muscles with the tips of her fingers, loving how solid he was and how strong. When she got to his still engorged staff, he caught her wrist in his hand. "If you want to get ready in time, you might not want to go there."

Oh, she wanted to go there, but Isabella sighed. "You're right. We have to get ready."

After they dried each other off, Isabella padded bare-footed across the Persian rug to her closet where the costumes Andre had arranged for them awaited.

Her dress was white silk, taffeta and lace, with black piping standing out in sharp contrast. Her hat was white with curls of white ribbon and black lace.

Ronin's costume hung beside hers. His outfit was all black velvet and lace. The blouse he'd wear beneath the jacket was made of black silk, and the tights were black with inlaid designs. The pointed-toed, patent leather shoes had two-inch heels, competing the ensemble.

Ronin's eyebrows twisted. "I'll wear everything but the shoes."

"But they go with the costume," Isabella protested.

"I can wear my combat boots. They'll match. They're all black."

Isabella shrugged. He hadn't balked at the rest of the costume. Why bother arguing over shoes. Especially if what he had, and was comfortable in, matched. She peeled the dress off the hanger and groaned at the accompanying petticoats and bloomers she'd have to wear beneath it. "This will take a while."

"Better get cracking." Ronin slapped her bare ass and laughed. Then he shook his head. "What goes first?"

Working together, they managed to dress each other, laughing and cursing along the way. By the time Isabella had done her hair and positioned her hat on top, it was time to go downstairs.

She walked out of the bathroom, placing her mask on her face to find Ronin, fully dressed in his velvet jacket, mask and a hat befitting one of the Three Musketeers crowning his head with a fluffy black ostrich feather curling toward the rear. Around his waist was a belt with a scabbard and a sword.

Isabella's heart fluttered. "You look magnificent."

"You're pretty hot, yourself." He gave her a low bow then straightened, offering her his arm.

Isabella slipped her gloved hand around his elbow, and they walked out of the bedroom together. "I want to check on my father before we go down." She led the way to her father's suite and knocked softly.

Andre opened the door.

"Is he awake?" Isabella whispered.

"Yes, of course, I'm awake," her father shouted. "But I might fire our butler if he does not stop pretending he is my mother."

Andre, stoic as usual, didn't bat an eyelid. "Your father would like to attend the ball." He spoke in a straightforward manner with no hint of sarcasm.

Isabella laughed. "My father is not the best patient."

"Yes, ma'am," Andre agreed. "Perhaps you could talk to him."

"No one needs to talk to me," her father groused. "All I need is help getting into my clothes."

Isabella touched Andre's arm. "I'll handle this." She turned sideways to get her skirt through the door and swept into the room. "Father, you promised."

"I did no such thing."

Isabella clucked her tongue. "You did. And if you go back on your word, I'll leave the ball and go into the streets to dance all night."

He stopped trying to sit up and glared. "You know it is not safe for you to be out in the streets during Carnival. What happened to me could just as easily happen to you." He held up a hand. "And don't tell me you can take care of yourself. I know that. But that man came out of nowhere. Neither Lorenzo or I anticipated what he would do. I am extremely lucky to be alive."

Isabella patted his arm. "I know, Papa. And I'd like you to stay that way. The doctor wanted you to rest and let your wound heal. It won't heal if you're downstairs bumping into people. Would you like to bleed all over them?"

He shook his head.

"Then stay in bed," she ordered, putting the same inflection in her voice she would use with a recalcitrant child. "I'll be downstairs...inside the house." She waved toward her dashing Musketeer. "Ronin will be at my side."

"The entire evening, sir," Ronin interjected.

Isabella's father continued to glare. "I worry about

you, Isabella. I should be the one down there. If someone wants to stab a Pisano, it should be me. Not you."

"No one is going to stab me, Papa." She smoothed her gloved hand over his arm. "I'll be fine. I have the best of the best watching over me."

Ronin slipped an arm around her waist. "I'll take good care of your daughter, Mr. Pisano."

"You'd better, or I'll leave this bed and teach you a lesson or two." He waved his hand, encompassing Ronin's outfit. "Just because you're dressed as a Musketeer, doesn't mean you're good with a sword."

Isabella's lips twitched, and she bit down hard on her tongue to keep from saying Ronin was very good with a sword. She was sure her father would not be amused.

His eyes narrowed. "You'd better take your fiancé out of this room before I run him through with that fancy sword."

"Oh, Papa." She bent over the bed and pressed a kiss to his cheek. "It won't be the same without you presiding."

"You will be perfectly lovely." He patted her hand. "Like your mother."

Her eyes burning, Isabella turned toward the door.

Ronin took her arm and escorted her out onto the landing.

Already guests had arrived, gathering in the front entrance, waiting to be introduced to the hostess of the ball.

"Ready?" Ronin asked, angling his head toward her.

Isabella nodded, her heart racing, her gaze scanning the faces she could see and the porcelain masks hiding the identities of others. For the first time since her family had sponsored the masquerade ball, the fun was gone and all she could think about was how sinister the masks appeared.

RONIN DIDN'T LIKE IT. The frivolity of Carnival had taken a turn that day in Piazza San Marco, going from fun-loving to deadly in a split second.

Any one of the guests tonight could be the man who'd paid the dead jester, or another one of his mercenaries.

To keep Isabella safe, Ronin would have to keep the guests far enough away from her without making her appear standoffish. If he had to, he'd take a knife or bullet for her to keep what happened to her father from happening to her.

Once they reached the bottom of the staircase, Ronin curled his arm around her waist and guided her toward the entrance where they would receive the guests.

Niccolo joined them, taking up a position on the other side of Isabella. He wore a dashing waistcoat in bright red velvet, trimmed in gold braid. With a warm smile, he added to the welcoming committee, smiling and talking to people as if he were part of the Pisano family.

One by one, the men and women greeted Ronin

first. He studied each person, searching for potential weapons.

A man dressed in a frilly, royal blue waist coat and wearing a wolf mask attempted to pass Ronin, moving directly to Isabella.

Moving quickly, Ronin stepped in front of him with his hand outstretched, ready to shake the man's hand or take him down, depending on what came next.

The man spoke in English. "Pardon me," he said, lifting the mask to expose a freckled face and red hair. "I can't see a bloomin' thing under here." The young man held out his hand and shook Ronin's. "Thank you for inviting us to the party. I promise to behave myself, as soon as I get rid of my mask." He winked, thanked Isabella and joined his friends near the musicians' dais.

Isabella leaned close to Ronin. "I think you scared the poor boy."

"Rather scare them than let them think you're fair game."

She snorted. "He's just a boy."

"And you're just one person. With so many around, you might not see the enemy coming until you have a knife buried in your belly."

Isabella's lips quirked upward. "Thank you for the bloody detail."

"If it keeps you on your toes, I've done my job."

She straightened, smiled at the next guest and shook her hand. Once she'd passed, she leaned toward Ronin again. "Really, you don't have to hover."

"I made a promise to your father."

"And you take your promises seriously." She curtsied

for a man dressed as Georgian dandy and allowed him to raise her gloved hand to his lips.

Ronin glared.

Behind the half-mask, the dandy winked and released Isabella's hand.

Isabella poked Ronin in the gut with her elbow. "Stop glaring. You are scaring people."

"I can't help it. I don't like it when other men kiss you."

"It was only a hand."

He shrugged. "First, it's a hand then it's an arm," he muttered. "Who knows where it will lead."

"To Hotel Eden?" She smiled up at him. "Seems you started with a hand."

"My point, precisely." He lifted her hand, turned it over and pressed his lips into her palm. Then he closed her fingers into a fist. "Save that as a promise for later."

A rush of people entered, bringing their banter to a stop.

Several times, Ronin stepped in front of a man or a woman getting too close to Isabella. He'd rather piss off them and Isabella than risk Isabella's life.

An hour and a half later, the number of new guests trickled to a stop, relieving Isabella of her duties in the receiving line.

"I need a drink," she said and moved toward the bar set up in the opposite corner from the musicians.

Ronin stuck to her like a magnet, using his body like a shield to get her through the throng of dancing, gyrating people. The band played a mix of old-fashioned waltzes and modern rock and roll. At that moment, it was rock, and everyone was in the middle of the room, bumping and grinding, flinging their arms in the air to the beat of the drummer.

To Ronin, the evening was a nightmare. To the guests, it was a great party, and they appeared to be settling in for the night, drinking enough alcohol to make them stupid.

Isabella asked for a glass of wine.

Ronin requested a bottle of water.

Isabella stared at him over her glass, her eyebrows rising above her mask.

He frowned. "What?"

"No wine?"

"I don't drink when I'm working."

She took a sip of the red liquid, some of it clinging to her lips and making him want to lick it off. "That's too bad. You must have had a few drinks before you asked me to dance two years ago."

"Why do you say that?"

"You have yet to ask me to dance now."

"Finish your wine, and I'll dance your socks off."

The music slowed to a hauntingly beautiful slow song. A song he remembered from the night they'd met. Ronin plucked the goblet out of her hand and set it on a nearby table. Then he pulled her into his arms and swept her out into the middle of the foyer.

Many of the younger people chose to sit out the slow dance, preferring the faster, rock songs.

Not Ronin, and not the other couples who knew it was a good time for a little belly-rubbin' to music.

Keeping an eye on the others nearby, Ronin held

Isabella close, his hands around her narrow waist. The dress kept him from sliding lower to cup her ass. "I liked it better when you dressed as a bandit in pants. This skirt is impossible."

"The better to tease you with," she murmured against his neck.

"Oh, it's teasing me. I'm wondering if the study is empty and how difficult it would be to get beneath all that fabric and make love to you on your father's desk."

"Mmm. I'm sure we could manage. But you saw what went under the dress. It's not just the dress and petticoat. There are pantaloons, as well."

"You're right. It's too much to deal with."

She leaned back, a frown denting her brow. "Since when is a US Navy SEAL not up to a challenge?"

His hand found hers, and he squeezed it gently. "Since never. Come on." He led her away from the dancers to the side of the room, aiming for the hallway and the study beyond.

"*Signorina Pisano*," a female voice called out.

Isabella stopped, bringing Ronin to a halt in his headlong rush to get inside her.

The servant who'd brought them breakfast and waited on the table stood in a doorway.

"What's wrong, Amina?" Isabella asked, and then switched into Arabic. The two women spoke in hushed tones for a minute, far too fast for Ronin to keep up. He picked up words like woman and bathroom, but not much more.

Amina turned and hurried away.

Isabella sighed and touched his arm, giving him an

apologetic grimace. "I have to go check on a woman who is ill in the bathroom. I might be a few minutes."

"I'm going with you," he said.

She laughed. "Only as far as the door. We have two bathrooms on this floor. One designated for women, the other for men." She smiled. "I'll be in the women's bathroom."

"I'm still going with you," he insisted.

She shrugged. "As you wish." She led the way, circling the large entryway and dodging revelers dancing again to rock music. The lighting dimmed, and a disco ball shone down on the party goers. Ronin blinked, and then realized he wasn't blinking, the disco ball was, making the room even more confusing. How could he keep Isabella safe in an environment as chaotic as a battlefield? Any moment, he expected to hear the popping sound of gunfire and the rip of a burst from a machine gun. He pressed his hands to his ears, trying to block out the music. But the lights continued to blink. "Can we turn off that confounded light?" he shouted over the noise.

"After I check on the woman, I'll see what I can do."

Ronin followed her, almost dizzy with the cacophony of light and sound.

Focus. He had to focus. Isabella's life depended on it.

They reached the other side of the big hall. Isabella led him down a short hallway with doors on either side. When she came to one marked with the universal sign of a woman, she paused. "I can handle myself. I spent a year in Syria. Trust me."

He frowned. "I trust you. It's everyone else I don't trust."

"I will leave the door open long enough to make you comfortable, but the women inside will be disconcerted if you march in like you own the place."

He nodded. "Don't be too long, or I'm coming in whether or not the women will be comfortable. I don't give a damn about their comfort."

Isabella smiled. "But I do." She touched his cheek and ducked into the bathroom, leaving the door ajar long enough for him to see inside.

As she'd predicted, there were other women standing in front of the mirrors, adjusting their wigs, masks, hair and whatever else women did in front of mirrors.

He couldn't see into the stalls, but Amina stood near one, wringing her hands.

Obviously, whoever was in the stall wasn't feeling well, and it worried the woman.

The door closed between them, leaving Ronin to wonder what was going on. If he heard even a peep out of anyone inside, he'd be in like thunder.

God, he hoped he didn't hear a peep. Then again, he hoped he did. If something bad happened.

Waiting sucked, especially in tights and a velvet waist coat. He'd give anything for his Ka-Bar fighting knife and an M4A1 assault rifle at that moment. He hoped the night didn't end in violence, but his gut was telling him something was looming.

CHAPTER 12

ISABELLA FOUND the woman in the bathroom, losing everything contained in her stomach. The stench was enough to make her want to heave, but she held her stomach and talked the woman off the floor and to the sink, where she helped her wash the ick off her face and applied a damp paper towel to her forehead.

She'd obviously had too much to drink. Thankfully, she'd purged a good portion of the alcohol from her body. She'd be okay after a good night's sleep.

Isabella sent Amina out to find the woman's friends and to order a water taxi to get the woman back to her hotel.

By the time she exited the bathroom, with the drunk leaning on her arm, Ronin was pacing the hallway like a bull in a ring.

Isabella would have laughed if she didn't smell so much like vomit. So much for making love in her father's study. She'd be lucky if they made love at all that night, the way things were going.

When she appeared, Ronin stopped pacing and hurried to her side.

She held up her hand to stop him. "I wouldn't get too close."

"Why?"

Isabella wasn't afraid to speak English in front of her guest. The woman only spoke Italian and German. "She has been projectile-vomiting for the past fifteen minutes. I think she has emptied her stomach, but I can't be sure."

Ronin shook his head. "Let me help."

"Are you sure?" She glanced at his outfit. "No use in both of us smelling like this."

"I've smelled worse." He bent and started to swing the swaying woman up into his arms.

"Go slowly, the motion might make her lose it again," Isabella warned.

As directed, he lifted her slowly into his arms.

The girl's head lolled as she passed out.

"At least if she sleeps, she will not be gracing you with the contents of her stomach," Isabella noted. "Hopefully, she will remain unconscious until you get her safely to a water taxi."

Her girlfriends gathered around Ronin, exclaiming about how strong he was to carry their friend and how heroic to save her from a "fate worse than death."

Isabella rolled her eyes and fought to keep from snorting in a very unladylike manner.

She followed the gaggle of females and Ronin

toward the front entrance that would lead out to the dock.

"Stay close," Ronin said.

"I'm with you," Isabella reassured him.

SHE WANTED to stop at the entrance and have Ronin pass on the duty of carrying the girl to one of the bodyguards pulling bouncer duty at the entrance. But they were busy checking bags and patting down women in big dresses to worry about one woman on her way out.

Besides, Ronin was already halfway to the dock before he stopped and turned back to wait on her.

"I can take care of myself," she said.

"I know you can. You survived a year in a hostile country. I'm sure you'll be fine in Venice for a few short minutes." He waited for her to catch up then added. "But just remember, it only took a few short seconds for someone to attack your father in broad daylight."

Isabella was fully aware of the truth of his words and kept a vigilant watch in all directions, studying the people still arriving by boat or on foot.

Ronin grinned.

She frowned. "What?"

"I keep forgetting you're a trained combatant. You'd kick ass if someone tried to jump you."

"Damn right, I would." She even managed to say it with an American accent.

A chuckle bubbled up Ronin's chest and exploded in a burst of laughter.

The woman in his arms lifted her head, stared at him through blurry eyes and dropped off again.

A water taxi pulled up to the dock and stopped. The drunk girl's friends climbed in first and waited while Ronin got in with their friend, laid her out on a seat and climbed back onto the dock.

Meanwhile, Isabella spoke with the driver and slipped him a wad of bills. He grinned and slobbered all over her, thanking her for her generosity and promising to help get the woman inside her hotel when they arrived. Eventually, the taxi driver pulled the boat away from the dock.

Isabella hooked her arm through Ronin's and walked back to the house, wishing she didn't have to go back inside with the loud music and crowd of people. She'd rather run away with Ronin to a quiet spot where they could be alone.

"Too bad we can't escape to Hotel Eden," Ronin said, as if echoing her thoughts.

She sighed. "If only I did not have this party to over-see. But I promised my father."

Ronin nodded. "And a promise, is a promise." They entered the house, passing the two bodyguards, Lorenzo and Matteo.

As soon as her eyes adjusted to the blinking disco ball lights, Isabella stopped and stared up at the top of the stairs. "*Madonna!*"

Her father, dressed in a pirate outfit, swayed unsteadily, holding onto the top rail with one hand and his wounded belly with the other. His face was white without having used any of the face paint preferred by many of the party goers.

"The man is stubborn beyond reason," Isabella muttered. She lifted her skirts and plowed through the throng, intent on getting to her father before he plunged down the stairs in a headlong fall and broke every bone in his body, not to mention tearing his stitches and possibly bleeding to death.

Amina ducked out of a hallway as she passed by. *"Signorina Pisano! Signorina Pisano!"*

Isabella slowed but didn't stop. "What is it, Amina?" she said in Italian.

"Two men slipped into the house, through the kitchen. They have guns. I think they mean to do harm to you and your guests."

Isabella's heart flipped. She spun toward her fake fiancé. "Ronin, get help and go with Amina. She says two men got in through the kitchen and are carrying guns."

His expression turned to stone. "Where are they now?"

"I don't know. Amina can show you. I have to get my father to his room before he kills himself or someone else does it for him." She ran toward the stairs, shoving people aside. If men with guns were inside the house, everyone there was in danger. But if they were only after her and her father, the sooner she got her father to safety the better.

RONIN, didn't like it. He wanted to stay with Isabella

and make certain she got to a safe place. But Amina was pulling at his sleeve, urging him to follow her toward the kitchen.

He glanced toward the stairs.

Isabella had made it through the crowd and was almost to the top.

Ronin waited until she and Andre moved her father through his bedroom door, and the door was closed, before he allowed Amina to lead him through the maze of hallways to the back of the house.

She slowed, pressed a finger to her lips and pointed toward a door.

He hadn't been through that door yet and wished he'd taken more time to explore the palatial mansion earlier that day. But it couldn't be helped now. If the two men were inside, he'd be outnumbered and outgunned.

"We need to get help," he said. What were the words he needed in Italian? Every lesson he'd taken escaped him now.

Amina shook her head. "*Non capisco.*" And she pointed toward the door, making motions with her hands like she held a machine gun, firing rounds.

He gripped her arms and pointed back toward the music and dancers. In a low, insistent voice, he told her, "Go get Lorenzo and Matteo." With a gentle push, he sent her back toward the party.

She stopped and shook her head. "*Non.*" Again, she pointed at the door and made the machine gun motion.

Ronin waved her on. "Go. Get Lorenzo and Matteo."

Amina remained rooted to the floor, her eyes wide, wringing her hands.

"Go!" Ronin stopped short of shouting.

The door beside him burst open.

Amina bolted.

Two dark-skinned, black-haired men dressed dark clothing lunged for him and dragged him back into the room.

Ronin fought hard, putting all his training to work, with the thought in the back of his mind to be on the lookout for chairs. He couldn't allow the two men to take him down.

One had a knife. The other had a rifle slung over his shoulder and a pistol with an attached silencer in his hand.

With the music so loud in other parts of the mansion, the silencer wasn't necessary. No one would hear the shots fired.

Ronin ducked, threw a punch into the belly of the man with the knife and performed a sidekick, knocking the handgun in the other man's hand across the room.

Before the attackers could regroup, Ronin caught the wrist of the man with the knife as he doubled over and yanked him forward, planting his knee in the guy's face. The crunch of cartilage and the spray of blood indicated he'd broken the man's nose.

Ronin wrestled the knife out of his hand and shoved the bleeder into the other man who was fumbling with his rifle.

The two men fell to the floor but scrambled to their feet.

Ronin was halfway to the door when he was jerked backward by the collar of his costume. He loosened his arms and let the coat slide free of his body.

The man who'd pulled it from his body flung it to the side and attacked Ronin, blood still streaming from his broken nose.

His buddy was pulling the rifle strap over his shoulder. If he got the weapon in front of him, it would be all over.

Ronin couldn't leave the room and let these two men get their shit together. He had to put a stop to their plans. Here. Now.

He flung himself to the ground and swept his legs to the side, catching both men at the ankles and sending them flying to land flat on their backs.

Rolling to his feet, Ronin kicked the man with the rifle full in the face. His head snapped back, and he crumpled to the floor, out cold.

His friend lunged at Ronin, catching him in the side and ramming him into the wall.

Ronin hit the paneling so hard the breath shot from his lungs. His attacker reared back to punch him.

Ronin ducked to the side.

The man's fist crashed into the wall, and he clutched it to his chest cursing in Arabic.

While the man nursed his sore hand, Ronin gave him something else to worry about. He hit him hard with a sidekick to the kidney.

The guy crumpled to the ground.

Again, he kicked him, this time in the face, knocking

him backward to land on his back, blood gushing from his broken nose.

Both men lay still. He checked for pulses. They were still alive, but they might not be still for long.

Ronin pulled the ties off the drapes hanging in the window and made quick work, tying their hands behind their backs and their ankles. If woke up, they wouldn't be going far.

He shrugged back into the costume coat then grabbed the rifle and the knife. Easing open the door, he peeked out into the hallway, wondering where Amina had gone and why she hadn't returned with Lorenzo and Matteo.

With a rifle and a knife, he couldn't just waltz through the party without someone stopping him or questioning him. And he couldn't claim they were part of his costume when he was supposed to be from the seventeenth century.

"Fuck it." He tucked the rifle beneath his long coat and slipped the knife into his pocket. He couldn't leave them in the same room with the attackers, and he couldn't leave them anywhere near partygoers, drunk on alcohol and whatever else might be floating around. Someone could accidentally pull the trigger and cause all kinds of craziness and death.

He had to get to Isabella and her father. If two men had found their way into the mansion, there could be more.

CHAPTER 13

"Now that you're back in your bed, stay there." Isabella sat on the side of her father's bed, frowning down at the rock in her life who, at the moment, was weaker than a kitten. She wanted to be back downstairs helping Ronin, but she had to be sure her father remained locked in his room.

"My apologies, miss," Andre said. "I turned my back for a moment to relieve myself and found your father dressed and heading for the party. I believe he might be a little high on his pain medications."

"All that matters is that he didn't fall down the stairs or tear open his stitches." And that he wasn't gunned down or knifed by whomever was trying to kill him. "Are you sure you can handle the rest of the night? Do I need to send Lorenzo up to tie him down?"

Andre shook his head. "I'll lock the door when you leave and sit on the man if he so much as wiggles."

"Good."

"I'm a grown man. I don't need a babysitter," her father mumbled.

"Yes, you do." Isabella smoothed a hand along his cheek. "Sleep now. You won't even remember getting out of bed in the morning."

"I most certainly will," he protested and then yawned wide enough to split his cheeks.

"Sure you will." Isabella chuckled. "Sleep, Papa. I need you to be well." She rose to her feet, intent on getting back downstairs. When she started to turn away, a hand reached out to capture hers.

Her father pulled her back to face him and smiled. "I love you, *mia bambina*."

"I love you too, Papa." She kissed his cheek and stepped away.

His eyes drifted closed, and soon the sound of his soft snores filled the room.

"Take care of him, Andre," Isabella said. "I can't afford to lose him."

"Stay safe, *Signorina Pisano*. Your father needs *you* just as much as you need him. He missed you while you were gone."

She exited the room and paused with her hand on the doorknob. "Lock the door behind me to keep others out. In fact, barricade the door with furniture. I don't want any unwanted visitors in my father's room."

Andre nodded. "I will."

She stepped through and pulled the door closed, waiting for the soft snick of the lock moving into place.

Amina stood nearby, her eyes round and her expression scared.

"Amina, where is Mr. Magnus?" Isabella asked in Italian.

"I don't know. He went into one of the rooms downstairs." She clutched her hands together and glanced over her shoulder as if expecting someone to come after her. "There were two men. One with a gun. I don't know, miss. I don't know."

Isabella heart leaped into her throat. She grabbed the woman's arms and shook her. "Where are they?"

"I don't know. I am so frightened."

"Show me." Isabella turned the woman toward the main staircase.

She dug her heels into the floor. "*Non*, miss. Not that way." Instead, she led Isabella to the servants' narrow staircase, leading down to the kitchen and the back of the house.

Isabella had played on these stairs as a child, and sometimes used them when she wanted a late-night snack from the kitchen. But not knowing what she would find at the bottom, lent a particularly ominous air to her former childhood playground.

Amina hurried down the stairs, leading the way until she neared the bottom. She stopped short, refusing to go further.

"Which room?" Isabella asked. "Where last did you see my fiancé?"

"In the hallway."

In a mansion the size of the Pisano estate, he could be in any number of hallways. She'd spend too much time searching. "Show me."

Amina shook. "I can't. They will kill me."

"Who will kill you?"

"The men with the guns." Amina crumpled against the bottom step, tears streaming from her eyes. "They will kill me. They will kill my family."

"I won't let them hurt you, but you have to take me to Ronin." Isabella gripped Amina's arms, stood her on her feet and shook her. "Show. Me. Now."

Amina sniffed loudly and stumbled into the nearest hallway then ran to the next corner and turned.

Isabella hurried after her. Because of the heavy layers of her dress, she wasn't as fast and had trouble making the corners. Soon, Amina was well ahead of her, and all she could see was the woman rounding the next corner.

The Pisano estate stood in the corner intersection of two canals. The side entrance was where the servants and deliverymen brought the groceries and other deliveries. Had the two armed men entered through that direction? If so, what had happened to the additional security personnel her father had hired for the event?

Frustrated with the costume, Isabella pulled off the headpiece and flung it to the side. She shrugged out of one layer of the outer garment, shedding at least five pounds of fabric.

She rounded the last corner where she'd seen Amina and ran into trouble.

Two black-haired, dark-skinned men grabbed her arms and hauled her toward the exit, speaking in Arabic. Her heart plummeted to the bottom of her belly. They'd found her. Al-Jahashi's reach had extended across the Mediterranean Sea to Venice.

Through her despair, she knew one thing as truth. These men would not be lenient. They were ruthless, especially toward women. Isabella knew she didn't have a chance, but she sure as hell wasn't going to go down without a fight. "Let go of me," she yelled. "Let go, or I'll scream."

They completely ignored her threats and continued to drag her through the tunnel-like hallway toward an arched exit.

Isabella fought and kicked, but couldn't get her feet past the skirt of her dress to make contact with her abductors. Yes, she could defend herself, but not in the movement-limiting costume.

Trapped in a prison of her own making, she dug her slippers into the smooth tiled floors. The slick soles couldn't gain traction to slow the men dragging her away.

When they reached the exit door and tried to carry her through, she waited until one of them had to drop his hold in order to get through the door.

With only one man holding her arm, she swung her feet up, braced them against the door and used her body to slam her captor against the doorframe.

He grunted but didn't go down. Still holding onto her arm, he backhanded her with his meaty knuckles.

Pain shot through her head and gray fog crept in around her vision. Her knees weakened, and she slumped against her attacker.

No. No. No.

Isabella tried to shake the fog from her brain. She shouldn't pass out.

Her survival depended on her keeping her wits about her.

Before she could get her feet back under her, she was dragged out the door and tossed like a sack of potatoes into the back of one of the many motorboats moored at the dock.

She scrambled to find her feet beneath the layers of fabric wrapped around her legs. Now that the men had released their hold on her arms, she had a brief window of opportunity to attempt escape.

By the time she was able to stand, the two men dropped down into the boat. One of them advanced on her, reaching for her arm.

Isabella grabbed his hand and pulled him toward her with a sharp jerk.

The man lost his balance, his body rocketing toward her.

At the last second, Isabella stepped to the side and let him crash into another seat, the upholstery cushioning his landing. He was up again in a flash.

Anger flashed over her captors' faces, and they closed ranks around her.

The boat had drifted away from the dock. Isabella could jump over the side and swim to another landing, or she could fight her way out of the situation.

Her hesitation cost her. The two men grabbed her arms. One of them snapped a pair of handcuffs on one of her wrists and dragged her down to a metal rail along the side of the boat where he snapped the other cuff.

He stood back and smiled menacingly.

Isabella tugged and pulled, but the railing was

securely affixed to the boat, and she was secured to the railing. She wiggled her hand, trying to pull it through the metal cuff, but the man had cinched it tight enough she couldn't pull her hand free.

The men laughed and turned away from her, one of them stepping behind the steering wheel. He started the boat and pulled away from the dock.

Isabella watched as they left all she'd ever loved behind.

RONIN SHOT out of the room with the two men who'd accosted him and raced down the hallway toward the party. With so many twists and turns, he had to rely on the raucous music to lead him to the grand entrance.

The blinking disco ball confused him and forced him to close his eyes for a second to force back images of previous battlegrounds, lost friends and horror. He needed to orient himself in the here and now.

Focus.

When he opened his eyes, he scanned the room in the strobing blinks of color, searching for Isabella. People danced in their outlandish costumes, gyrating to rock music, completely unaware of the drama unfolding.

Ronin's gaze shifted to the staircase, praying she was still with her father, safely locked in his room.

He shook his head and pushed his way through the crowd. Knowing the kind of person Isabella was, she couldn't stay in her father's room for long. She'd have gone in search of the men with the guns to protect her guests and Ronin from harm.

God, he loved the woman, but she could be bull-headed, just like her father.

Once he reached the stairs, he took them two at time, arriving at the top breathless. At Marcus Pisano's room, he skidded to a stop and pounded on the door. "Bella!"

A voice could barely be heard from the other side. "She's not in here."

"Andre?"

"Yes, sir," the butler responded, sounding closer.

"Is Mr. Pisano okay?" Ronin pressed his ear to the door.

Andre's muffled voice came through a little more clearly, "He's sleeping. I have the door barricaded to keep him safe."

"You're not just telling me that? You're not being held hostage, are you?" His words sounded stupid even to his own ears. Would the people holding him hostage allow him to own up to being held?

"I promise you, sir, the only one holding me hostage is Mr. Pisano."

Ronin's gut told him that Andre was telling the truth. He had relied on more than one occasion on instinct. He hoped it was correct this time. "Where's Isabella?"

"I was hoping she'd found *you* by now."

"I'm going to look for her. I need you to call the police. Let them know I left a couple of men tied up in one of the rooms downstairs. And don't open this door until Isabella or I come back and ask you to."

"Yes, sir."

Ronin ran for Isabella's room, just in case she'd ducked in to change out of her heavy dress.

The room was as they'd left it earlier. He saw no indication she'd been there since.

Back out onto the landing, he bent over the railing and stared down into the mass of people celebrating Carnival at the masquerade ball. Several women had white gowns, but none of them were Isabella.

Then he spotted Amina, leaning against a wall, semi-concealed in the shadows of a hallway. She clutched her hands together, and her body appeared to be shaking.

Ronin couldn't be sure. The blinking lights made everything in the room appear to be shaking. But then everybody in the room was shaking to the music.

The lights, the music, the blinking made Ronin's head throb. He staggered down the staircase, struggling to keep the rifle concealed. He didn't want to ditch it, in case he needed it. With little patience remaining, he pushed his way through the crowd to where he'd last spotted Amina. She wasn't where he'd seen her.

With nothing else to go on, he ran down the hallway she'd be standing in. "Bella!" he yelled.

He couldn't have heard a response past the noise of the music behind him, but he kept running, his chest tight. Fear for Isabella squeezed the life out of his heart. Where was she? "Isabella!"

A movement down a branching corridor made him turn and follow. Soon he came upon Amina.

She lay hunched over on the floor, her body shaking. "Amina, where's Isabella?"

The woman shook, and her sobs could be heard over the thrum of the bass drum.

Ronin lifted her up by the arm, careful not to drop the rifle beneath his coat.

She turned her face to the side as if afraid he'd hit her.

He loosened his tight grip on her arm and struggled to find words in Italian. *"Dove è Signorina Pisano?"*

Amina's face crumpled, and tears spilled down her cheeks. *"Lei è andata."*

Ronin couldn't be one hundred percent sure, but he thought the words meant *She is gone.*

A lump knotted in his throat.

No.

"No," Ronin said. "Where is she?" He gave up trying to speak and understand Italian. Turning the woman around, he gave her a gentle shove. "Miss Pisano. Go."

Amina seemed to understand what he wanted. She stumbled forward, got her feet under her and led him through the maze of corridors, past one that led to the kitchen.

Niccolo stood just inside the door, talking with the chef.

Ronin ground to a stop. "Costa, have you seen Isabella?"

The man spun, clapping a hand to his ruffled collar. "You startled me."

"I'll do more than startle you if you don't answer me." Ronin stood taller. "Have you seen Miss Pisano?"

Costa shook his head, his eyebrows coming together in a frown. "Why? Is something wrong?" He stared at Ronin's rumpled, bloodstained costume and the bulge where he ineffectually hid the rifle he'd pilfered off his earlier attacker. "What happened to you? And where did you get that gun?"

"Jumped by two armed guys. I got the gun off one of them. Where were you?"

His face grew pale. "I've been coordinating additional menu items with the chef. I can't believe all this was happening without me knowing."

"I have to find Isabella. I think she's in danger." He turned back to follow Amina.

"I'll help." Costa fell in step behind Ronin.

He hoped the man didn't get in the way. He hadn't shown any sign of being useful in a fight.

Amina was several feet ahead of Ronin, waving at him, urging him to follow.

He did, wishing he hadn't wasted time questioning Costa.

The Syrian refugee ran through an arched doorway that led outside to a dock. She stopped and pointed at a boat disappearing around a corner. "Bella!"

Ronin caught a glimpse of the skirt of a white gown before the boat was gone. Someone had gotten to her and was taking her away.

Several boats were moored to the dock below him. He jumped down into one, then over to another searching for keys.

"Are you going to steal a boat?" Costa asked.

"I'm going to borrow one. Do you have any other

ideas?" Ronin shot back at the man. "They're getting away with Isabella. I'll do whatever it takes. Make yourself useful. Find one with the keys in it."

"Yes, yes, of course." Costa leaped into another boat on the other side of the dock and a moment later shouted, "I found one!"

Ronin hauled himself back up on the dock, tossed the rifle into the boat and dropped down beside Costa.

When he went to push the man aside, Costa blocked him. "I know the canals, do you?"

Damn. The man had a point. "Do you have the balls to push the limits of this boat and the waterways?"

Costa nodded. "I used to drive jet boats. Let me do this."

"I don't care who drives, just follow that boat before it gets away." Ronin held his breath and sent a prayer to the heavens as Costa turned the key. The engine fired up and roared to life.

Amina untied the line and threw it into the boat but stayed on the dock. "*Allahu akbar.*"

Ronin did a double-take, but couldn't spare the time to process the woman's comment. He had to get to Isabella.

Costa spun the boat around and pushed the throttle forward. The little craft leaped ahead and slid sideways as they rounded the corner where the other boat had turned.

The canal ahead was empty but for a gondola with a man poling along at a leisurely pace, singing to a couple kissing on the seat in front of him.

"Faster," Ronin urged Costa.

Costa edged the throttle forward, creating a wake that rocked the gondola and sent the man poling into the water. He came up cursing in Italian.

Ronin was sorry for the man, but he'd live. He wasn't so sure Isabella would. He prayed they weren't too late. As they passed one canal intersection after another, his hope of finding Isabella dwindled until, finally, he spotted a boat passing beneath an arched bridge. In the back of the boat was a woman wearing a big white dress with black trim

"There!" Ronin pointed down the canal.

Costa nearly hit the side of one of the buildings making the turn, but he corrected the steering, missing the brick by a hair.

Ahead, the boat with Isabella disappeared in the shadow of the bridge.

Costa pushed the little boat as fast as it would go, slowly gaining on the other boat.

By the time they passed beneath the bridge. Ronin could see Isabella clearly. She seemed to be tied to the boat railing, and she was tugging hard, trying to dislodge the railing or get out of whatever was tying her down.

It was at that moment, one of the two men in the boat noticed they were being followed. He lifted is hand and pointed it at Costa.

"He's got a gun!" Ronin said. "Duck!" He didn't wait for Costa to react, he placed his hand on top of the man's head and shoved him down.

Costa's hand was still on the steering wheel as he went down, causing their boat to swerve sideways.

Ronin yanked the throttle back in time to keep them from smashing into a wall.

Gunfire echoed off the walls of the surrounding buildings.

"Keep low but drive," Ronin commanded. "I have to get Isabella off that boat."

"Are you crazy? They're shooting at us!" Costa shouted.

"I don't give a damn if they're firing RPGs, we're getting closer, and you're going to drive or move the hell over and let me."

"I'll drive," Costa said, his voice shaking as badly as his hands. "Just make them stop shooting."

Ronin retrieved the rifle from where he'd flung it earlier, hunkered low and moved toward the front of the boat. If Costa could get him close enough... What? He'd shoot the man with the gun? What if he hit Isabella?

He could throw himself in front of the man shooting at them, but that would just get him killed, and he'd be of no use rescuing Isabella, and Costa didn't have the balls or training to do the job.

Ronin wasn't sure what his plan was, but he had to be ready when an opportunity presented itself.

The shooter unloaded several more rounds, the bullets hitting the sides of buildings, the boat and the windshield, shattering the glass.

Costa had to look around the shattered windshield to see where they were going. Thankfully, he was closing the distance between the two boats.

If he got close enough, Ronin might have a chance to shoot the gunman without hitting Isabella.

He lifted his head enough to see over the bow.

The gunman fired three rounds, the first going wide, the second hitting the windshield behind Ronin and the third splintering the railing an inch away from Ronin's ear. He ducked lower.

Suddenly, the shooting stopped.

Ronin raised his head.

The gunman had dropped the clip from his handgun and was fumbling in his pocket, presumably for another.

Opportunity had just presented itself.

"Steady!" he shouted to Costa, as he rose in position, rested the rifle against his shoulder and sighted in on the man who'd been shooting at him.

Isabella must have seen what he was doing and flattened herself against the side of the boat, giving him as much clearance as possible.

As the man shoved the next magazine into the handle of his pistol, Ronin pulled the trigger.

The shooter stood for a second longer as if frozen, and then slumped sideways, falling into the boat driver.

The boat swerved sharply toward a wall. At the last minute, the driver corrected, but it was too late.

The boat listed sideways and turned over in the inky canal water with Isabella tied to the rail.

CHAPTER 14

Isabella knew she was in trouble when the boat rose up on its side and flipped upside down. She only had seconds to haul in a deep breath and hold on to keep from breaking her wrists, before she was plunged into the fetid waters of the Venetian canal.

She fought with renewed purpose to break free of the rail or the cuffs, to no avail. If she couldn't get out of it the cuff while high and dry, her chances of getting free now were even slimmer in the dark, cold water.

Hoping the cool water would shrink her hands enough to slip them through the cuffs, Isabella pulled but soon gave up. The cuffs had been tightened so much she couldn't get them over her hands. Her only hope was to reach a pocket of air and hold on until Ronin could rescue her.

Since she was close to the rail, she couldn't get to the center of the boat which would be the highest point in the water and might possibly contain a bubble of air trapped when the boat flipped.

She stretched her neck, praying she could reach any pocket of air. Her lungs burned with the effort to hold her breath, the need to suck in more overpowered her. At that moment, her forehead came up into an air pocket. She tipped her head back enough for her nose to clear the water. She released the air she'd held in her lungs for what felt like forever through her mouth and inhaled through her nose. She could barely fill her lungs with the boat tilted and sinking deeper.

She tipped back her head again. The bubble had shifted and she couldn't find it. She moved around frantically searching for it or another pocket of life-giving air, her heavy dress hampering her efforts and drawing on her energy to fight its strangle-hold on her body.

Soon, she had no more air nor strength. She stopped fighting and drifted toward the silty bottom of the canal.

So, this was how she would die. Though she'd done her best in Syria and freed a lot of women, she hadn't accomplished all she'd wanted in her lifetime. Regrets welled up inside her as she floated in the darkness, her lungs burning from the need to release old air and draw in new. She wished she could have become a mother, her own mother having taught her how to love unconditionally and with all her heart. And her father...he would be devastated upon learning of her death and would probably die of a broken heart. But most of all, Isabella regretted she hadn't told Ronin she loved him. The man was everything she could have wanted in a partner for life. He was funny, kind and incredibly strong. He didn't want to dominate her but to protect her and be with her for as long as they had together. Which happened to be not that very long.

She prayed he would go on with his life, meet another woman and have children. He would make a good father; he'd be just and fair. And he'd love his children deeply and without reserve. He was just that kind of man.

If she got out of the canal with her life, she'd walk away from being Isabella Pisano in a heartbeat if it meant being with Ronin. Sure, she'd have to learn to get by on a lot less and probably get a job. Work never hurt anyone. Look at her father. He'd worked all his life to build a corporation that would provide for himself, his family and many more families.

If only she could be so successful.

Thoughts drifted through her mind as water filled her lungs. Death wasn't nearly as painful as she'd imagined. She relaxed and let it take her.

"Go! Go! Go!" Ronin yelled.

Costa raced the boat up to the capsized one and yanked back the throttle. The craft drifted closer, slowing considerably.

Before they even came to a complete stop, Ronin shrugged out of his costume jacket and dove into the water near to where Isabella had gone under. He was careful not to dive too deeply, not knowing what he'd find in the canal, or how shallow it might be.

Night and the murky water hampered his effort to find the only woman he'd ever loved. He couldn't see anything. All he could do was feel his way.

He found the back of the boat, the propeller and the ladder. Running his hand along the corner, he worked his way around to the side.

The water exploded in front of him as the boat driver surfaced, gasping for life-giving air. When he saw Ronin, he lunged toward him, hefted himself out of the water and came down on Ronin's head with the force of a water buffalo.

Ronin went under without fighting, grabbed the man's waistband and took him down him, dragging him toward the bottom.

The man kicked and fought, desperate to get back up to breathe.

Ronin didn't let him. Instead, he twisted the man around and climbed up his back, pressing his hands on the guy's shoulder to keep him under.

The driver struggled, swinging his arms, his legs and twisting his body.

Ronin locked his arm around the man's neck and held tight. In his Navy SEAL BUD/S training, he'd been the trainee who could hold his breath the longest. But he didn't have time to outlast the driver. He needed to get on with the business of saving Isabella before she drowned. With a quick twist, he snapped the guy's neck and pushed him away.

After surfacing quickly for air, Ronin continued his search for Isabella.

It didn't take long to find her. He ran into her dress

first and followed the hem up to her waist and finally her face. She was so still. God, was he too late?

She'd been tied to the railing when he last saw her.

Running his hand down her arm, he came across what was holding her to the rail. Handcuffs—one cuff clamped to the rail, the other around Isabella's wrist.

Without anything to break the chain, the cuffs or the rail, he could do nothing to bring Isabella to the surface.

Ronin kicked free of her and surfaced.

Costa was at the edge of the boat he'd been driving about to dive into the water.

"Wait!" Ronin called out. "Throw me my costume waistcoat."

"What?"

"Just do it!" Ronin yelled.

Costa retrieve the garment and leaned over the side of the boat, handing it to Ronin.

Ronin dug in the pocket and sent up a prayer of thanks. The knife he'd stashed earlier was still there. He dove down and hacked at the chain between the two cuffs.

The more he hacked, the longer it took, and the more desperate he became. Finally, the links broke. Isabella was free.

He hooked his arm over her shoulder, across her chest and under her opposite arm and swam to the surface.

"You found her," Costa exclaimed.

"Yeah, but she's not breathing." With all of his strength, he dragged her to the nearest landing and pulled her up onto the surface. Her dress was heavy, making the process ten times more difficult.

Rolling her to her side, he used the knife to cut the strings cinching her corset. He then used his finger to open her mouth.

Canal water trickled from beneath her lips.

Then he laid her on her back, pinched her nose with his fingers, covered her mouth with his and filled her lungs with air, watching to see that her chest rose with each breath. Four breaths, and he paused to check for a pulse.

Nothing.

He moved his hands to her chest and began compressions. "Come on, Bella. You can't quit on me now. Pisanos are stubborn. They aren't quitters." He pumped a few more times and bent to fill her lungs with air again.

"Breathe, Isabella," he said into her ear. Again, he checked for a pulse. Was that a nudge against his fingertips? "Come on, Isabella. Live. I can't do this life without you."

He forced more air into her lungs and checked her pulse. It was there and beating stronger.

Suddenly, she coughed and gasped, sucking in a ragged breath.

Her eyes opened, the streetlight hanging over the landing shined light on her face. She smiled and raised a weak hand to his cheek. "You found me."

And then she passed out.

A siren blared nearby, growing louder as a police boat rounded the corner and came to a halt.

In halting Italian, Ronin explained what happened.

The police called for assistance and an ambulance boat arrived soon after.

Within moments, they had Isabella loaded on a backboard, wrapped in warming blankets and stowed in the boat.

Ronin started to step into the boat with her, but the medic who spoke English held up his hand. "Only family members are allowed to ride with the patient."

"Does a fiancé count?" he asked. No way would they leave without him. He'd hang on to the outside of the boat if he had to, but Isabella wasn't going anywhere without him.

The man said something to his partner in Italian. He turned back to Ronin and shrugged. "You can come."

"What about me?" Niccolo stood on the landing, holding the line for the borrowed boat.

"Get back to the Pisano estate," Ronin said. "Let Andre know what's going on. Isabella's father will be beside himself when he wakes."

Costa nodded and sighed. "Thank you for saving *Signorina Isabella*. She means the world to her father."

And to me, Ronin thought.

The ambulance boat ran with the lights flashing and the siren blaring all the way to the main landing where Isabella was transferred from the boat to a wheeled ambulance.

Ronin wasn't allowed to ride in the back with her, but he rode shotgun with the driver, ending up at the same hospital Mr. Pisano had been to earlier that same day.

The medics disappeared inside with Isabella, giving Ronin heart palpitations until he was allowed to go back and be with her.

She was hooked up to a heart monitor, cannula for oxygen and an IV. They'd stripped her of the costume, replacing her clothes with a hospital gown.

"I bet that dress gave them hell," he murmured.

A nurse adjusted the dials on the monitors and turned to smile at him. "*Signorina Pisano* has been given a sedative. She might not wake until morning."

"I can stay?" he asked.

"*Si.*" The nurse showed him how to use the call button and told him she'd be on duty until early the next day.

As soon as the woman left, Ronin lifted Isabella's hand and pressed it to his lips, his eyes burning with unshed tears. He'd come so close to losing her. A tear found its way out of his eye and down his cheek.

Isabella blinked and squinted up at him. "Am I alive, or are you my angel?"

He laughed and brushed the moisture form his cheek. "Bella, I'm no angel."

"Then I'm alive." She sighed, closed her eyes again and slept.

Ronin settled in a chair beside her bed and watched her, afraid that if he didn't, something would happen. She might slip away. He knew it was ridiculous, and the monitors would alert him and the nurses, but having almost lost her once...

An hour after he arrived, a knock sounded on the

door, and Andre stuck his head through. "How is the *signorina?*"

Ronin stood and stretched. "Resting." He frowned. "Who's keeping an eye on Mr. Pisano?"

"When Lorenzo and Matteo heard what happened to *Signorina Isabella,* they cleared the guests from the house and helped *Signor Costa* and the police clear out the two men you'd left tied up in one of the sitting rooms."

"And Amina?"

"We called a doctor to give her a sedative. She confessed she'd been threatened by al-Jahashi's men. If she didn't let his gunmen into the house, they would kill her mother and sisters in Syria."

Ronin shook his head. "Does she realize how close Isabella came to dying?"

Andre's lips thinned into a straight line. "She won't be working for *Signor Pisano* after tonight. *Signor Costa* fired her. Though remorseful, she didn't quite understand that trading one life for another would solve nothing."

His fists clenching, Ronin drew in a deep breath and let it out. "Mr. Pisano?"

"Is sleeping like a *bambino.* Now that he knows Isabella is safe. The effect of the painkillers has leveled out, and he's resting peacefully. Lorenzo is standing guard until my return."

"What happened to the security detail on the back door?" Ronin asked.

Andre's jaw tightened. "The police found them in the canal. "Thanks for coming to check on Isabella, and for filling me in on what's going on.

"Security is on high-alert, and the estate is in lockdown," Andre reported.

"Good. Isabella will be glad to hear that."

"If you can see to *Signorina Pisano's* safety, I need to get back and check on *Signor Pisano*."

"I won't be leaving her side for even a moment," Ronin assured the butler. "Tell me, Andre, you're not just a butler, are you?"

The man squared his shoulders, coming to attention. "No, sir. My mother was Italian, my father a member of the British Army. I grew up in England and joined the Army straight out of school. I'm a former member of the British Special Air Service."

Ronin smiled. "I should have known." He held out his hand to the man highly trained in special ops. "I've worked with a few of the SAS. They were good men. We'll have to talk when we're not saving the world one Pisano at a time."

Andre nodded then shot a glance at Isabella. "I'll be at the Pisano estate if you need me."

After Andre left, Ronin had more time to think about what had occurred. One thing was clear, al-Jahashi's thugs were as ruthless in Venice as they were in Syria. The ISIS leader had to be stopped.

A COUPLE HOURS LATER, Isabella stirred, opened her eyes and asked in a hoarse voice, "What happened to my dress?"

Ronin had been pacing the floor, afraid to get too comfortable and fall asleep. As far as he was concerned, as long as al-Jahashi had a price on her head, Isabella was still in danger.

He crossed to her bedside and lifted her hand. "They cut you out of it."

"Good," she croaked. "I'll never wear another."

Ronin chuckled. "If you want to wear pants to our wedding, I have no problem with that." He raised her hand to his lips and kissed it. "If you want to show up in your underwear, it's okay with me. If you want to come naked, I'm on board." He waggled his eyebrows.

Isabella smiled and winced, her eyes closing. "On board. That reminds me...what happened? Seems you were aiming a rifle at the boat I was in." She opened her eyes. "By the way, where did you get a rifle?"

Ronin filled her in on all that had happened since she'd gone upstairs to rescue her father. From the two guys who'd jumped him to hacking her free of the boat and performing CPR, he spilled the details of their evening. "And you thought Carnival would be boring," he said, shaking his head.

"Is that why I feel like I was run over by a truck?" she asked.

He nodded and bent to press his lips to her forehead. "I never should have left your side."

She shook her head. "If you hadn't taken care of the guys with the gun and knife, they might have gotten to my father, or taken it out on the guests. You did the right thing."

"But I almost lost you," he whispered hoarsely.

"I'm alive because of you." She squeezed his hand

holding hers. "You were there when I needed you most. I knew you'd find me in time."

"I'm glad you knew, because I wasn't so sure."

She pressed his palm to her cheek. "There's something I want to do before I die."

"But you're not dead, and you're not dying," he assured her.

She chuckled and coughed. "I know. But when my life passed before my eyes, I had one big regret, and I want to rectify that before anything else happens."

He loved the feel of her soft skin beneath his hand. If she weren't in the bed, covered with wires and beeping monitors, he'd gather her into his arms and hold her close. When he'd seen that boat flip, Ronin had never been more scared in his life.

He swallowed to dislodge the knot forming in his throat and whispered, "What do you want to do before you die, sweetheart? Go skydiving? Sail around the world? See the Aurora Borealis? You name it, I'll make sure it happens."

"Nothing so exhausting." She cupped the back of his hand in hers and pressed a kiss to his open palm. "I wanted to tell you that I love you."

Ronin's knees melted, and he almost fell to the floor. "That's what you thought about while you were drowning?" He shook his head. "Bella, those are the sweetest words I could ever expect to hear." He lowered the rail on the side of her bed, lay down beside her and gathered her in his arms, wires and all. "Sweetheart, I'll do whatever it takes to deserve your love."

"You don't have to do anything," she said, closing her

eyes and with a smile curling her lips. "You just have to be you."

"You want me to leave the Navy, I will. If you want me to find a job in Italy, I'm there."

"No. Please, don't quit the Navy and your position with the SEALs. I know how much it means to you and how it's a part of who you are. I'm just afraid whoever sent those men to capture me will be back again. I'm sure they went after my father to get to me. I couldn't live with myself if my father died because of what I did in Syria." She became agitated, the heart monitor pulsing faster with every beat of her heart.

Ronin leaned up on his elbow. "Shh, Bella. Don't worry, we'll think of something."

He smoothed his hand over her hair and calmed her.

When Isabella fell back into a troubled sleep, a plan formed in Ronin's mind.

CHAPTER 15

Two weeks later...

"Magnus, we're in place, ready when you are," Maddog's voice said into Ronin's headset.

"Roger." Ronin adjusted the tripod on the front of his rifle, lining up the barrel with where he expected to engage his target.

His team had moved into position after dusk. Darkness had settled on the village, the stars just beginning to appear and shed light on the buildings below.

Ronin lay at the edge of the roof, staring through his rifle sight at the building intelligence had identified. The heat of the day had already begun to dissipate, cooling the sweat on his brow. If their sources were right, Abu Ahmad al-Jahashi had used this structure as his headquarters for the past week. He and his terrorist fighters had taken this village from the locals without much of a fight.

What could they do? They were unarmed and too poor to afford the luxury of having an opinion about politics. All the villagers wanted was to be left to tend their goats, grow their crops and live in peace.

ISIS had taken their village, most of the food they'd stored for winter and whittled their herds of goats down to a paltry few animals.

For a small bribe, they'd been more than willing to share information about the ISIS leader's movements to the intelligence guys embedded in a nearby community.

"Vehicle approaching," Viper said from his position near the road leading into the small hamlet built into the side of a hill in Syria.

The sun had set more than an hour ago, giving them plenty of time to get into position and prepare for the ISIS leader's return to his base.

Ronin kept his rifle completely still and turned his head to study the SUV entering the narrow streets.

"That looks like the vehicle the intel guys reported he'd be in," Viper said. "They said he stole it from a village mayor he murdered."

They'd also confirmed he'd let his men rape the women and small girls before he killed every member of the mayor's family.

The bastard had no shame, no heart and no soul. It would be a privilege for Ronin to put him out of the world's misery.

He settled in behind the sight and waited for al-Jahashi to step out of the SUV. Ronin had chosen to infiltrate the village alone, slipping past the guards positioned on either side of the road leading into the walled community. He'd rappelled in from the cliff side and chosen a position on a rooftop close enough to ascertain the identity of his target, and yet far enough away to give him enough of a head start to get out of town when things got hot.

Helicopters waited a couple miles away, loaded for bear, ready to provide air support if necessary, and extraction when needed.

Ronin had insisted on going alone. It was easier to get one man inside undetected than an entire team. As soon as he dispatched al-Jahashi, he'd slip back out as quietly as he'd come in, no one the wiser as to who had taken out one of ISIS's most violent leaders. He hadn't come for the glory or to get his name in the papers. He'd come to take care of the people he loved. And he'd promised Isabella he'd return alive, not in a body bag.

Had they gone through regular channels, it would have taken a literal act of Congress to deploy the SEAL team. As it was, Ronin made a few calls, found out others had been studying the al-Jahashi situation, and the timing couldn't have been better to stage an operation to take out the ISIS leader.

The SUV appeared in Ronin's sights and pulled to a stop, brake lights gleaming red before the driver shifted into park.

The passenger door opened and the interior light shone on the man climbing out.

In Ronin's sight, the image couldn't have been clearer. The man had dark, thick eyebrows, a full dark beard and the distinguishable scar slashed across his right cheek.

"I have my mark," Ronin whispered, curling his finger around the trigger.

"We've got your six," Maddog said.

Ronin gently squeezed the trigger. The silencer on the end of the weapon muffled the sound of the shot fired. The bullet hit the mark, but al-Jahashi stood as if surprised. For a long moment, Ronin waited, ready to fire again, if the first round didn't do the trick.

Al-Jahashi dropped to his knees and then fell face-first to the ground. The men around him scrambled in an attempt to understand what had just happened.

Quietly, efficiently, Ronin grabbed his rifle and leaped over the side of the building to the ground, scaled the wall of the village and dropped to the other side without being seen.

Shouts rose up from inside the village, but Ronin was already several yards away, running up the hill, heading for the other side.

"I'm out," he reported.

"Bringing up the rear," Viper acknowledged.

"Covering your asses," Maddog weighed in.

"Mission accomplished?" Viper asked.

"Mission accomplished," Ronin responded, already at the top of the hill. Keeping low to the ground, he tried not to present too much of a silhouette on the ridge. ISIS terrorists would be searching the village, and then the surrounding areas, looking for the sniper who'd killed their leader.

Ronin planned on getting out of Dodge before the bad guys knew who'd hit them.

Behind him, he heard the faint footsteps of his colleagues scrambling up the hill. He glanced back to see Maddog and Viper making their way back to the same helicopter pickup point Ronin aimed to reach before anything else happened. The choppers were on the way in, the familiar *whomp-whomp-whomp* of rotor blades beating the air and giving him a sense of urgency to get where he was going in a hurry.

As he topped the ridge, he dropped to the prone position and covered his team as they scrambled the rest of the way up the hill.

The mission had gone without a hitch. In fact, it had gone entirely too smoothly. Ronin's gut knotted. His instinct was telling him something wasn't right, but he couldn't put his finger on it. Maddog, Viper and the rest of the team made it over the ridge with no problem and nobody shooting at them.

Ronin watched for a few moments longer, scanning the rugged hillside bathed in starlight. Nothing moved, no one was chasing them.

He could barely see the headlights of the SUV. The walls of the village hid them. But a faint glow was moving toward the entrance.

He moved his night vision goggles into place over his eyes and studied the exterior of the walled village and the rooftops.

He could see the familiar green heat signature of someone moving around the top of the building from which he'd staged his target acquisition. The man appeared to be looking toward the building where al-Jahashi was killed. Then he turned to face the direction the SEALs had exited.

Time to go.

Ronin slipped over the ridge and half-ran, half-slid down the other side.

A Black Hawk helicopter from the 160th Night Stalkers landed long enough for the team to climb aboard. Another hovered nearby, providing cover in case ISIS managed to move fast enough to send someone out to fire on them. Once everyone was in the first craft, it lifted into the air.

The chopper had only halfway turned when something slammed into the tail section and sent it spinning out of control.

Ronin had barely gotten aboard and didn't have his safety harnessed engaged.

The helicopter plummeted toward the ground, whirling like a wound-up top, centrifugal force flung Ronin out the door. By then, the Black Hawk was only ten feet off the ground. But when he hit, pain shot through his leg, and the wind was knocked out of his lungs.

The chopper landed hard, the blades still turning, but it was intact.

For the first few seconds, Ronin couldn't move, couldn't breathe and couldn't call out to his buddies. All that was going through his mind was he would be breaking his promise to Isabella. He wouldn't be coming home.

Then as if a switch was flipped, he sucked in a deep

breath, replenishing his lungs and fueling his body with the determination to live. He'd be damned if he broke his promise.

Ronin tried to get up. Pain stabbed through his leg, and he fell back to the ground. He ran his hands over the leg and bit down hard on his tongue when he encountered a protruding bone. Compound fracture.

Damn.

The pilot of the second Black Hawk opened fire, launching two laser-guided Hellfire missiles. The resulting explosion shook the ground beneath Ronin.

SEALs and pilots scrambled from the disabled helicopter. Some helping others who'd been injured in the rough landing.

Ronin had been thrown at least a hundred yards from where the bird had landed. The others would spend too much time searching for him and risk having the second chopper shot down. If he wanted to be rescued, he had to help himself.

He pushed himself up to his knee, jolting the broken leg, but fighting through the pain. On the count of three, he hopped up on his one good leg, the pain in the other making black spots swim before his eyes. Ronin waited until the pain and the spots cleared enough he was fairly certain he wouldn't pass out, and he could see where he was going. Then he started the painful journey toward his team, hopping, one foot at a time, every movement sending crippling pain throughout his body.

When he was within fifty yards of the chopper, a member of his team ran toward him, slung his arm over his neck and half-walked, half-carried Ronin toward the chopper. Another SEAL jumped down and helped load him in and lay him on the floor next to his best buddy Maddog, and Frito, the Hispanic SEAL who always had a joke and laughed in the face of danger. Doc, the team medic, was working on Maddog, establishing an IV and cutting open the man's pant leg.

Doc glanced across at Ronin. "Status?"

"Compound fracture, left leg," Ronin said through the gritted teeth.

"Let me get Maddog stabilized, and I'll be with you next."

"No worries." Ronin glanced up at Viper. "Is he going to make it?"

Viper nodded toward Maddog. "Maddog is. But Frito..." he shook he head. "Fell from the helicopter right before we crashed. The skid hit him in the chest, crushing him. It took all of us lifting, to get him out from under."

Ronin's chest hurt almost as much as if he'd been crushed beneath the chopper. "He had a wife and kid."

Viper nodded.

Another reason why SEALs shouldn't marry.

Was he being selfish to wish that kind of life on Isabella?

Doc finally made his way over to him, got him hooked up to an IV with Viper holding the bag, shot a little morphine into the drip and waved at him. "Say goodnight, Magnus."

Already loopy, Ronin let the drug take effect. "Goodnight, Mag—" and he was out.

ISABELLA HAD FLOWN from Venice to Frankfurt as soon as she'd gotten word from Ronin's brother, Sam. Ronin was at Landstuhl Regional Hospital near Kaiserslautern, Germany. Lorenzo had come along as protection.

She'd had to run the gamut of red tape to even be allowed into the military hospital, since she was an Italian citizen, even though she was Ronin's fiancée. Until they were married, and she had a military dependent ID card, she'd continue to have problems.

Ronin's brothers Sam and Mack met her in the lobby and helped her through the forms and paperwork.

"I thought Ronin had three brothers," she said as they finally headed for the elevator.

Sam grinned. "We told Wyatt not to come. He's still on his honeymoon." He shrugged. "Besides, it's just a broken leg."

Isabella nodded, though her gut tightened. A compound fracture could have killed Ronin, had it severed a major artery. From what she'd been told, he'd been thrown from a helicopter. The fall alone could have ended his life.

"He's lucky he didn't break his fool neck," Mack said.

Isabella's thoughts, exactly.

Sam chuckled. "Probably landed on his hard head."

Isabella understood the need to laugh off an injury. There were enough frightening events and sadness in the world. If someone came out of a bad situation, it was better to laugh than cry.

She also knew one member of the team hadn't been as lucky. Maybe she was insensitive, but she was glad it hadn't been Ronin.

Finally, they reached the door of Ronin's room.

Her heart fluttering, her breath catching in her throat, Isabella pushed open the door and entered.

"Look who we found wandering around in the lobby?" Sam said.

Ronin opened his eyes and turned his head toward the door. When he spotted Isabella, he frowned. "What's she doing here?"

Mack's brow rose. "Uh...fiancée?" He looked around as if for the punchline. "That's what they do. They come to the hospital when their soldier or SEAL is injured." Mack grabbed Sam's arm. "We were just going for a cup of coffee. You two look like you need some alone time to talk."

Ronin raised his hand. "Don't...go. What I have to say can be said in front my brothers."

"Think about it, Bro. You're still on pain meds," Mack warned.

"I'm thinking more clearly than I have in a while." He faced Isabella. "I'm sorry. But I can't marry you."

Isabella's heart lodged in her throat. She couldn't lie. The words stung. But she also knew he didn't mean them. He was probably worried about his ability to recover and hold a job.

Though he'd spoken to her, he wasn't making eye contact.

She glanced at Mack and Sam. She didn't have to say a thing.

The two brothers nodded and backed out of the room.

"Going. For the coffee," Sam said. "Be back in a few."

Once the door closed behind the brothers, Isabella crossed to the bed and reached for Ronin's hand.

He jerked it back. "I'm serious. It's over."

Fear turned to anger, and Isabella crossed her arms over her chest. "Look at me, Ronin Magnus," she commanded in her best Angel of Mercy combat voice.

He shook his head. "You know as well as I do that nothing between us will ever work. Why kid ourselves?"

She could see the hopelessness in his face and hear it in his voice. He didn't want to end their relationship any more than she did.

Instead of trying to talk her way out of it, she took a risk and tried reverse psychology. "You're right."

His head snapped up, and he finally looked at her, a little shock in his eyes at how easily she acquiesced. As quickly as the shock appeared, it disappeared into a fierce frown. "Damn right, I'm right. Navy SEALs should never marry."

She nodded. "I'm sorry about your teammate. I'm certain his wife is grieving and wishing she'd never married him."

"Exactly. Now she has to raise their daughter alone. Pile on the grief, and it makes for a miserable way to live."

"Yeah. I'm sure she would rather not have loved him than to have known love for the few years she had him. How selfish of your friend to do that to her. I'm sure he didn't explain it in a way that she would understand."

Ronin's eyes narrowed. "He told her from the beginning what could happen."

"And she still agreed to marry him and have his children? Silly woman." Isabella tsked her tongue. "She'd have been better off alone. No one should fall in love, especially if the person they love could be killed in a war."

"No, she could have been married to a civilian who didn't run the risk of being killed in a war."

She turned away and paced to the window. "No, it's just not good to fall in love with anyone. You never know when a bus is going to hit them, or the car they're driving will run off the road, or the boat they're in will flip and drown them." Isabella spun and pinned Ronin with a tight glare.

"I think the woman is trying to make a point," Ronin said, a frown still darkening his gaze but his lips quirking.

That was the man Isabella remembered and fell in love with. The one who could look at a situation and find something funny about it. The man who could make her laugh and see the beauty in life. Not the one trying to push her away because he was afraid to love her, but more afraid she'd love him.

She went to him and took his hand in hers.

When he tried to pull it free, she held on. "Ronin, we don't know how long we have on this earth. We can't second-guess our decisions based on what *might* happen. We have to go with our hearts. She pressed his hand to her chest where her heart was beating fast. "My heart is telling me to take a chance. True love doesn't come along often in life. I didn't think it would ever happen to me—until I met you. Now, I can't think of anyone I'd rather spend whatever time I have left on this earth with. If we get to grow old together, great. If we only have a year together, a month, a day, an hour, I'll take it. You make me happy. I'll take all the happy I can get for as long as you let me."

His hand tightened in hers and pulled her fingers to his lips where he dropped a kiss. "What if I die on a mission?"

"Then you will die knowing I love you and always will. I'm strong. I'll survive, and my memories of our time together will keep me going."

"What if we have a child?" He swallowed hard before continuing. "What if she grows up without a father?"

"I'll tell her every day what a great man you were and how proud he'd be of the strong woman she will become." Isabella raised his hand to her cheek. "Please. Don't give up on us. We found each other after two years apart. It has to mean something."

For a long moment, he stared up into her eyes, his own suspiciously moist.

Isabella held her breath, praying he'd see how right she was. "I would come to live in Virginia. We can get an apartment near Little Creek. I can get a job."

He snorted. "Someone's bound to need a female mercenary or spy. They'll be knocking on your door." Ronin shook his head. "You can live anywhere you want, now that al-Jahashi is dead. My people tell me that faction has scattered. No one has stepped up to take over as a leader. I'm sure they have more pressing needs than revenge on a woman who killed a dead man's brother."

Isabella nodded, thankful the threat had been neutralized.

"You'd give up your life in Venice?" Ronin asked.

She nodded. "For you." Isabella gripped his hand harder. "For us." She hurried on, "And maybe, when you retire from the Navy, you could work for my father, and we can split our time between the U.S. and Italy?" Isabella pulled her bottom lip between her teeth. She'd never wanted something as badly as she wanted a life with Ronin. "Or not. We can live wherever you want."

"I wouldn't want your father to hire me just because I'm family."

Her heart fluttered. Was he thinking a life together would work? "My father told me he'd hire you the day you leave the Navy. He needs people he can trust."

"You've been thinking about this, haven't you?"

She nodded, her eyes stinging. "Every day. I know what to expect, being in a relationship with a Navy SEAL. It doesn't scare me."

His lips curled into a smile. "I don't think anything scares you. I love that about you."

"You're wrong. I am scared of one thing."

"And that is?" he prompted.

"Losing you before we have had a chance to be together." She turned his hand and pressed a kiss to his open palm.

"Bella," he said, his voice clear and soft.

Her knees always weakened when he called her Bella. "Yes, Ronin?"

"I'd get down on one knee and ask you properly, but...well...I can repeat the performance when this damned leg is mended." He slapped his sheet-draped leg and grimaced. Then he straightened and took her hand in his. "What I want to say is...even though we're engaged, though, for the record, I never asked you... would you marry this broken-legged Navy SEAL? I promise to love you until the day I die, hoping that will be a very long time down the road. I'll come home to you when the Navy lets me, and I'll protect you to the best of my ability when I'm in town. Otherwise, you're going to be on your own."

She pressed a finger to his lips, and then bent until her mouth hovered over his. Her heart swelled with a happiness so complete she would take every bit of it she could handle, and more, for as long as it lasted.

No regrets.

She whispered against his lips, "Yes." Then she kissed him.

Enjoy other military books by Elle James

Hearts & Heroes Series
Wyatt's War (#1)
Mack's Witness (#2)
Ronin's Return (#3)
Sam's Surrender (#4)
Brotherhood Protector Series
Montana SEAL (#1)
Bride Protector SEAL (#2)

Montana D-Force (#3)
Cowboy D-Force (#4)
Montana Ranger (#5)
Montana Dog Soldier (#6)
Montana SEAL Daddy (#7)
Montana Ranger's Wedding Vow (#8)
Montana Rescue

SAM'S SURRENDER

HEARTS & HEROES SERIES BOOK #4

New York Times & USA Today
Bestselling Author

ELLE JAMES

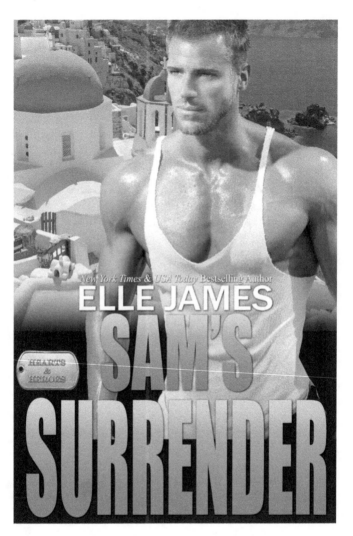

New York Times & USA Today Bestselling Author

ELLE JAMES

HEARTS
&
HEROES

SAM'S
SURRENDER

CHAPTER 1

SAM STARED down at the Thira airport landing strip on the Greek island of Santorini, his fingers biting into the armrest of his airline seat.

In the air, he preferred to be the pilot, and that the aircraft be the Blackhawk he flew for the Army. In fact, he'd rather be with his unit, the 160th Night Stalkers, ferrying Special Operations teams to the hot spots of Afghanistan, Iraq and Syria, than at the mercy of an island-hopping, fixed-wing pilot who got his flight status from a cereal box. Based on the hard landing, Sam wondered how many hours the pilot had under his belt, or if he'd ever been in the Navy performing land-ings on an aircraft carrier.

The thought of spending two weeks staring at the crystal-clear waters of the Mediterranean Sea and the shockingly white buildings of his vacation location made his teeth grind. What the hell was he going to do for the entire time? The inactivity would make him batshit crazy. He lived for his team, for the Army, and for the next mission.

His commander called him an adrenaline junkie, always looking for his next high. Maybe Colonel Cooley was right. So what? Someone had to pilot the helicopters into and out of war-torn areas.

Sam didn't have a wife and kids to go home to. Why not let him ferry in the real bad-asses to complete their missions?

His commander's response had been, "Magnus, you're pushing the limits, getting too close and scaring the crap out of your passengers."

"And the fact they're going into firefights isn't frightening enough?"

The CO pointed a stiff finger at him. "Exactly. Those Spec Ops dudes have enough on their minds. They don't need some rotor-head making them upchuck before they have to sling bullets at the enemy."

"That SEAL shouldn't have been on my bird. He had the flu."

"The flu, hell. You were popping in and out of those hills like a prairie dog in heat. What did you expect those guys to do? Half of them were hurling chunks. The point is, you're taking risks and not keeping the souls on board in mind while you're doing it." Colonel Cooley pushed back from his desk and stood. "Flying is not all about you. It's about the goddamn mission."

Sam stood in front of the CO at attention, taking his chewing out. Yeah, he probably deserved it. But hell, he was the best pilot in the unit. He could fly circles inside the circles around the other Black Hawk pilots. He tried to calm his commander by stating, "Sir, I promise to do better."

"Damn right, you will. But that's not enough. Other members of the unit, and I, have noticed you're wound entirely too tight. If you don't learn to relax, you'll explode like forty pounds of C4."

"Sir, I'll take it easy."

The colonel's lips formed a thin, tight line. "Yeah." The CO resumed his seat behind the metal desk. "You're scheduled for leave starting tomorrow, correct?"

"Yes, sir," he said. "I'm attending my brother's wedding in Ireland. I'll be gone four days, max."

"Wrong."

Sam's head jerked back. "Sir?" He stared at his commander, a frown narrowing his eyes. "I had this leave approved months ago. But if you can't spare me, I'll call and tell Wyatt I can't make it."

"I didn't say you weren't getting your leave. You're attending your brother's wedding, and then you're taking an additional two weeks of leave to chill out, wind down and fucking get a grip on your nerves, your attitude and your life."

His stomach lurched as if he'd been sucker punched. "But, sir, I'm needed here. I'm the best damn pilot you've got."

Colonel Cooley shook his head, his lips twisting into a frown. "You might have the best skills, but right now, you're a loose cannon, and a danger to yourself and the people you're supposed to be helping."

"You can't be serious," Sam raised both hands. "I

haven't taken that much time off in years. I wouldn't know what to do with myself."

The CO glanced up at him without speaking for a full thirty seconds.

Sam began to sweat. Even he knew he'd crossed the line, questioning his superior officer's judgment. He clamped his lips tight and waited for the additional ass-chewing to come.

"I'm as serious as a heart attack. And, if I'd been in the chopper on your last flight, I might have *had* a heart attack."

When Sam opened his mouth, the CO held up his hand to stop him.

"If two weeks' leave isn't enough to get your head on straight, I'll have to ground your ass. Don't make me to it."

Sam's gut clenched. Ground him? That would be a fate worse than death. What would he do if he couldn't fly? Flying was his life. Flying defined him.

Too shocked to say another word, Sam stood like a stone statue.

"Get out of my sight for two weeks and four days. When you return, I'll determine whether or not you're ready to fly again. I suggest you take the time to get your shit together. Go for a walk, find a beach, get laid, meditate...whatever you need to do to figure out how to calm down." He waved toward the door. "Now, get the hell out of my office."

Sam popped a salute, executed a sharp about-face and marched out of the office.

That had been five days ago. He'd been to Ireland for

his brother Wyatt's wedding, which had ended up being more stressful than flying into enemy territory. His brother Mack's girl had been targeted by Irish gypsies after she witnessed one of them murder another guest in the wedding hotel.

The visit turned into a nightmare. For a while there, Mack and his sweetheart had been touch-and-go in a ploy to flush out the Travelers and squelch their attempt to kill them.

What had happened in Ireland had not made for a good start to his enforced R&R.

The pilot taxied the airplane to the terminal and stopped.

As soon as the seatbelt sign blinked off, Sam punched the release on the metal buckle, stood and grabbed his go bag from the overhead bin.

And waited, tapping his fingers on the back of the chair in front of him. The sooner he was off the plane and on terra firma, the quicker this nuisance of a vacation could begin. Today was D minus fourteen.

The ground crew took what felt like forever to push a flight of stairs up to the fuselage, but finally, the cabin door was open and the passengers filed out.

The setting sun glared into Sam's eyes and a salt breeze ruffled his hair. He blinked and shaded his face until he entered the terminal. Again, time dragged until he cleared customs. He kept his military ID tucked away in his wallet. No use alerting anyone to American military in the area. Terrorists existed in every corner of the world. As the crow flew, Santorini wasn't that far from the troubles plaguing the Middle East.

He'd booked a bed and breakfast room on a hilltop overlooking the whitewashed city. From looking at the map, he gauged the distance was a good walk, mostly uphill, from the airport. He could use the exercise and decided to skip a taxi and stretch his legs.

The sun slipped into the ocean as he slung his bag over his shoulder and set off at a quick pace, inhaling the salty air and wondering what activities were available on a dinky-shit island.

He should have stayed on the mainland of Europe where he could hop a train to anywhere he wanted. But no, the dart had to land on Santorini. Perhaps his method of picking destinations was flawed.

Maybe he'd find a bar and drink himself into oblivion for the next two weeks. What else was there to do?

KINSEY PHILLIPS HAD SPENT her day off snorkeling in one of the many picturesque coves Santorini had to offer. The au pair gig she'd landed came at the perfect time and, so far, the job wasn't hard at all.

The Martins had been nice, if a little stand-offish, and their two children were well-behaved and quiet. Kinsey tried to get them to open up, but she figured she was still too much of a stranger for the kids to trust her.

She wasn't too worried. The family was supposed to be on Santorini for a full month. That would give them time to get to know her. By the end of the month, they'd love her and beg to keep her on as their permanent nanny.

And, if a month was all she had, at least she'd earn enough money to purchase her plane ticket back to the States.

Her first time in Europe had been nothing if not fraught with drama, but everything seemed to be working out. Finally.

She'd sold all her furniture, emptied her bank account, pulled up all her stakes and moved to Greece to take a job as an assistant manager of a hotel in Athens. With a one-way ticket, she'd boarded a 777 and left her crappy love life behind.

Her heart full of dreams and hope for the future, she'd landed, eager to start her new job and try her skills at speaking Greek.

The job had fallen through upon arrival. The hotel had been bought out by a competitor, and she'd been let go before she even started. Not too deterred, she'd decided to spend a couple weeks in Athens, maybe find another job or just enjoy a short vacation. Two days into her stay, she was mugged. Thieves had taken her backpack with everything inside—her money, laptop, cellphone, passport and credit cards.

She had no parents to call and bail her out, or friends she could count on back in Virginia. In her last job, she'd been the secretary to an elderly gentleman who had retired and moved to Cabo San Lucas. Kinsey had no backup.

Broke, with no way to pay for her room, food, a plane ticket home or even a phone call, she'd sat on a bus bench and cried.

That's when Lois Martin sat beside her and quietly asked what was wrong.

Kinsey had been so happy to hear someone speak English, she'd poured out her troubles to the stranger.

An hour later, she had a job offer, a plane ticket to Santorini and a taxi ride to the U.S. Embassy to get a replacement passport. In just that short amount of time, her life was back on track.

Now that she'd been in Santorini for a week, she was beginning to feel downright optimistic. She smiled as she climbed the hill to the hotel where she and the Martins were staying and where she occupied the adjoining room next to their suite.

The concierge nodded as Kinsey entered the hotel. "Good evening, Miss Phillips. I have a message for you." He handed her a sealed envelope.

The Martins often left notes for her at the concierge, informing her of their dinner plans and whether she should join them. "Thank you, Giorgio." She tore open the envelope and slipped free the note card. "Did you get to see that sunset? It was beautiful."

"Haven't been outside the hotel since I got here this morning."

"Such a shame. But then, I imagine all the sunsets are as pretty here on Santorini." She glanced down at the card. *Meet us at the Naousso Café at eight.* "What time is it?" she asked.

"Fifteen minutes to eight o'clock," he replied.

Her heart skipped a beat. She didn't have much time to change and get to the restaurant. "I'd better get going."

"I'm glad you've enjoyed your stay," Giorgio said. "Will you be leaving soon, as well?"

Why would he ask if she was leaving? When she'd told him a week ago that she'd be there for a month. "No, I'll be here for another three weeks."

The concierge frowned and opened his mouth to say something, but a woman approached him with questions about nearby restaurants.

Kinsey smiled, waved and stepped into the elevator, wondering if Giorgio had misunderstood her when she'd first said she would be there for an extended stay.

She got off on the third floor, ran her key card over the lock and pushed through the door into her room.

She dropped her beach bag on the floor and stepped out of her skirt cover up before heading for the bathroom. Her bed had been made in her absence. An envelope lay on the pillow with a wrapped chocolate resting on it. The staff had been wonderful, treating her just as well as they did the Martins, even though she was the au pair.

Kinsey stripped and entered the shower. Using the shampoo provided by the hotel, she washed the salt out of her hair and off her skin, and applied a liberal amount of conditioner.

Five minutes later, she was dry. Dressed in a short black dress with a matching shawl and low heels, she strode past the empty concierge's desk. By now, Giorgio must have gone home to be with his family.

With only a few minutes to spare, Kinsey headed out of the hotel, hurrying through the winding streets to the café they'd frequented on several occasions. Though it had decent food, Kinsey didn't think the restaurant was quite up to par with the Martins' luxurious lifestyle. But they seemed to like it and were friendly with the owners.

Darkness settled around the Greek island, and lights lit many of the corners. Kinsey usually walked with the Martins to the restaurants. This trip was the first time she'd ventured out at night on her own. The children usually didn't go to sleep until after ten, and Kinsey didn't know anyone else on the island, so she hadn't been interested in exploring the nightlife.

Gathering the light shawl around her shoulders, she tucked her purse beneath her arm and stepped out smartly. She was careful not to let her heels get caught in the cobblestones as she wove through the streets and corridors between the buildings.

She hurried past the shadowy corners and alleyways, a creepy feeling spreading through her senses. Several times, she slowed her pace and glanced over her shoulder, swearing she'd heard an echoing set of footsteps. But when she paused and listened hard, she didn't hear anything but the sounds of voices from nearby homes and buildings.

Shrugging, she moved on.

Almost at the top of the terraced hillside, she heard the footsteps again. This time, they were real, and they came fast from behind her.

Kinsey stepped to the side, to allow whoever was in such a hurry to move past her on the narrow stairs. She glanced over her shoulder and waited for the owner of the footsteps to pass.

Two men in dark clothing appeared from around the corner below, wearing dark hats pulled down over their foreheads which shadowed their faces.

A trickle of fear pulsed through Kinsey. She was a lone female in a strange land. Two of them had appeared, and they were big and burly. But they appeared to be in a hurry, as if they were late for something.

They came at her, taking the steps two at a time.

Kinsey thought better of waiting for them to pass and continued her ascent, hoping to reach a better-lit area with more people around in case she ran into trouble.

But the more she climbed the twisting stairs, the closer the men came, until they almost overtook her.

She'd just decided to move aside again when she was hit in the back hard enough to send her sprawling onto her hands and knees, sliding down several steps before she stopped. "Hey, watch it!" she yelled. Her heart banging hard in her chest. *No. This can't be another mugging.*

Before she could rise to her feet and face the man who'd knocked her down, a meaty hand wrapped around her arm and yanked her to her feet. "Let go of me," she demanded and fought to break the hold on her arm.

The other man clamped a hand over her mouth, pressing a cloth over her nose with a sickly-sweet scent.

Kinsey twisted in an attempt to free herself of the man's iron grip and the cloth making it hard to breathe. But her muscles weren't cooperating, and her vision blurred. No. She couldn't pass out. She had to stay awake and find a way to escape her attackers. This outrage was not happening to her.

But it was.

As the darkness crept in around her senses, the cloth was removed. Once she could breathe fresh air, she tried to call out, but the feeble attempt at a scream came out as a pathetic murmur. "Help...me." She was lifted and thrown over the man's shoulder. Kinsey couldn't even raise her head or kick her legs.

All the self-defense training she'd taken before leaving the States did her no good when she couldn't control a single muscle. She flopped like a ragdoll as her captor ran up the steps to the main road.

ABOUT THE AUTHOR

ELLE JAMES also writing as MYLA JACKSON is a *New York Times* and *USA Today* Bestselling author of books including cowboys, intrigues and paranormal adventures that keep her readers on the edges of their seats. With over eighty works in a variety of sub-genres and lengths she has published with Harlequin, Samhain, Ellora's Cave, Kensington, Cleis Press, and Avon. When she's not at her computer, she's traveling, snow skiing, boating, or riding her ATV, dreaming up new stories. Learn more about Elle James at www.ellejames.com

Website | Facebook | Twitter | GoodReads | Newsletter | BookBub | Amazon

Or visit her alter ego Myla Jackson at mylajackson.com
Website | Facebook | Twitter | Newsletter

Follow Me!

www.ellejames.com
ellejames@ellejames.com

ALSO BY ELLE JAMES

SEAL's Seduction (#6)

SEAL'S Defiance (#7)

SEAL's Deception (#8)

SEAL's Deliverance (#9)

Ballistic Cowboy

Hot Combat (#1)

Hot Target (#2)

Hot Zone (#3)

Hot Velocity (#4)

Texas Billionaire Club

Tarzan & Janine (#1)

Something To Talk About (#2)

Who's Your Daddy (#3)

Love & War (#4)

Hellfire Series

Hellfire, Texas (#1)

Justice Burning (#2)

Smoldering Desire (#3) TBD

Up in Flames (#4) TBD

Plays with Fire (#5) TBD

Hellfire in High Heels (#6) TBD

Cajun Magic Mystery Series

Voodoo on the Bayou (#1)

Voodoo for Two (#2)

Deja Voodoo (#3)

Cajun Magic Mysteries Books 1-3

Billionaire Online Dating Service

Hostage to Thunder Horse (#1)

Thunder Horse Heritage (#2)

Thunder Horse Redemption (#3)

Christmas at Thunder Horse Ranch (#4)

Demon Series

Hot Demon Nights (#1)

Demon's Embrace (#2)

Tempting the Demon (#3)

Lords of the Underworld

Witch's Initiation (#1)

Witch's Seduction (#2)

The Witch's Desire (#3)

Possessing the Witch (#4)

Stealth Operations Specialists (SOS)

Nick of Time

Alaskan Fantasy

Blown Away

Warrior's Conquest

Rogues

Enslaved by the Viking Short Story

Conquests

Smokin' Hot Firemen

Love on the Rocks

Protecting the Colton Bride

Heir to Murder

Secret Service Rescue

High Octane Heroes

Haunted

Engaged with the Boss

Cowboy Brigade

Time Raiders: The Whisper

Bundle of Trouble

Killer Body

Operation XOXO

An Unexpected Clue

Baby Bling

Under Suspicion, With Child

Texas-Size Secrets

Cowboy Sanctuary

Lakota Baby

Dakota Meltdown

Beneath the Texas Moon

Printed in the USA
CPSIA information can be obtained
at www.ICGtesting.com
LVHW021027130924
790975LV00004B/39